Penny Ante: The Good, the Bad, and the Romance

by

Shelley White

In for a Penny, Book Four

Dedication

Thank you to all my Penny readers. Turns out the magic isn't quite finished with me or Penny's family.

Forward

Have you ever heard a writer say that her characters wouldn't leave her alone or that they insisted their story be written? While that may have been the case for my first three Penny books, it's not true now. Penny no longer speaks to me; her and Tripp's story is over. Happily ever after. The end. But the *magic* wasn't done with me.

After over two hundred years, the magic had become invested in the women in Penny's family and the love lives of Elizabeth's descendants. When Penny & Tripp's daughter, Mabel, is dumped by yet another loser, it was the last straw.

Now, the old magic has a life of its own and it isn't following the rules.

Prologue

Sam found Mabel in the tree house, where she always went when she was upset. They played there a lot, too. His parents' favorite place to go was Gypsy Falls to visit Auntie Penny and Uncle Tripp. He always got stuck playing with Mabel, but she mostly wasn't so bad.

He poked his head up through the door hole in the floor. "Why're ya hidin' up here?"

Mabel sniffed. "They don't even know I'm gone. All everyone cares about is Auntie Kate and Uncle Greg's new baby."

Sam frowned. "That's not true. Your mom told me to find you to play and she'd call us at dinner." He crawled over to sit next to Mabel on the mat she kept up there.

"I'm not important," she wailed.

"Are so. You're the oldest. That makes you in charge of Bertie and the new baby. You have to show 'em how to act. That's important."

She peered at him through wet lashes. "I'm not older than you."

"I'm a boy. I'm supposed to be older. 'Sides, I'm not in your family." He puffed out his chest.

"Ya huh. You belong to Auntie Bobbie and Uncle Peter."

"They're not your *real* aunt and uncle, just friends. Your auntie Kate is your dad's sister. My parents aren't

1

related to yours." Being older meant being smarter, too.

Mabel scrunched up her forehead. "So we could get married since you're not my real cousin."

Sam scooted to the edge of the mat. "Nuh uh! I'm never marrying no girl!"

Mabel giggled. "Oh, so you're going to marry a boy?"

Sam's jaw dropped. "No! I'm never marrying nobody. Gross!"

"Whatcha gonna do, then? How will you have babies?"

"Boys don't have babies." Of this, he was confident.

Mabel rolled her eyes.

"I'm going to be a pirate, anyway. Can't have a girl or a baby on a pirate ship." Sam was glad to see Mabel was cheering up, even if it was at his expense. "Come on. Let's play book until dinner."

Mabel crawled over to a trunk and opened the lid. She pulled out several picture books before finding the one she wanted, *Pi-rah-tees of the High Seas*. "Let's do the pirate one. I'll show you a girl can be just as good as a boy on a boat."

Sam pulled rudimentary costumes out of another trunk and tossed Mabel an eyepatch and plastic cutlass. He tied a red bandana around his head and donned a tattered black vest.

"Sam, do you ever wish we could really go into a book like in the stories Mom tells?" Her one-eyed gaze sad.

"You know those are just made-up stories? Magic isn't real."

She sighed. "I know. It'd be neat, though. Think of all the places we could go."

Sam pointed a plastic dagger at Mabel. "Ahoy, me hearty! We be heading to a desert island to dig for treasure. What more adventure do you want?"

Mabel clashed her cutlass against the dagger. "Aye, aye, first mate, Earvin. Hoist the main sail and batten down the hatches!"

Sam groaned. Ever since Mabel learned his middle name, Earvin, after Earvin "Magic" Johnson, she used it at every opportunity. His first name, after Samuel Clemens, wasn't near as embarrassing. "You scurvy dog, I'm nobody's first mate. I'm the captain of this here vessel."

"It's hard to be captain if you're swimming with the fishes. Walk the plank!" She fell to the mat in a fit of giggles and Sam followed. "Thanks for coming to cheer me up, Sam. No matter how many more babies come, you'll always be my best friend."

"You're my best friend, too. So long as I don't have to marry you."

****

A couple years later...

Mabel's curly head popped up through the floor opening. "What are you doin' up here?"

Sam turned from her. "Go away."

She climbed all the way up and plopped into a sagging beanbag chair. "It's my tree house. You haven't been over in forever. I see you less now that you live next door."

"Can't a man have a few minutes to himself?" Sam grumbled.

Mabel snorted. "You're nine."

"Nine and a half," Sam said, not meeting her gaze.

"Sam, what's wrong?" She crawled over to where

he sat in the cabin's other depleted bag seat.

He shrugged. "Nothin'. Just wanted to be alone."

"Well, you picked a dumb place for it. As soon as Bertie's show is over, she'll be out lookin' for me."

"All the more reason for you to leave."

She planted herself cross-legged in front of him. "Not until you tell me why you're sad. We're still best friends, aren't we?"

"I can't be best friends with a girl. Mike is my best friend now."

Mabel's lip quivered.

Darn it. He was the one who was upset. Why did he always have to make her feel better? He sighed. "You're my best girl friend." His cheeks warmed. "I mean, you're my best friend who's a girl."

"You're still my best friend, but only because I'm mad at Hannah right now. Usually, you're second." Disaster averted, she returned to her usual pain-in-the-butt self. "Now you have to tell me what's wrong. I'm probably better at solving problems than Mike."

Sam slumped farther into his seat. "Not this one. Mike already knows and can't fix it either...I didn't make the team."

"Which team?"

"Farm League. Cuts were today. Mike made first baseman. My dad is going to be so mad."

Mabel climbed in to share Sam's seat. "No he won't. I've never seen Uncle Peter mad at anyone."

"But he's so great at sports and I play like dookie. This was my last hope. He'll be disappointed."

"Baseball's not your thing. So what? There are lots of other sports."

Sam peered at her over the rims of his glasses. "I

sprained my finger playing basketball. I sprained my ankle playing soccer. Mom's afraid to let me try football. She's probably afraid I'll sprain my brain. It's the only thing that seems to work on my whole body."

"You're good at horseback riding."

"That's not a sport."

"Is so!"

"I mean, it's not a sport I can do in school. I'm not even as good at it as you."

"Duh. I ride Polly almost every day. We'll figure out something you can do. Probably something without balls."

Sam snickered.

"What?"

"Nothing. Big kid stuff." Sam put on a superior air.

"Whatever. Come on, let's play book."

"I'm too old for that baby game."

"You're not too old to sulk up in my tree house." She raised her brows in challenge.

"Fine. But no baby books." He lowered his shoulders in defeat.

Mabel jumped up and scurried over to the trunk. She pulled out a slim paperback that Sam suspected exceeded her reading level. "This is an adult book."

Sam eyed it skeptically. "What's it about?"

"It's called a paranormal romance." She vibrated with excitement.

"I'm not reading a romance. Gross. Where'd you even get it?" He took it from her and looked at the cover. "*Chase the Night*. Sounds dumb." He tossed it back in the trunk.

She pulled out another one. "This one says it's a mystery. It looks old. We can read till we find out what the mystery is, then pretend to solve it."

"I suppose." He took the book from her. "Mabel, where did you get these books?"

She flushed. "They were just in a box."

"And where was the box?"

"In the back of the closet. I only took these two. The rest were too old or too boring-looking. I didn't mess up any of the papers or letters." Her chin jutted out in defiance.

"Fine. We'll do this *Pom Squad Mystery* thing, but you have to promise to put both books back when we're done."

"Promise." She criss-crossed her chest with her pointer finger. Smiling, she opened to the first page. "Oh, look! Basketball."

Sam groaned. "This is the last time."

****

Several years later…

Sam stood at the base of the Kinney tree house and yelled up. "Mabel, are you up there?"

"No."

"Come down or I'm coming up."

"I'm not here. Go away."

"Mabel, get your ass down here or I'll tell your mom the dog was innocent of the toothpaste incident of 2018."

"Don't you swear at me, Samuel Earvin Celansky, or I'll tell your mom why your brother's closet door fits cock-eyed." She sighed. "We could do this all day. Just go home. It's not your business anyway."

"We do appear to have reached a stalemate."

"Who even talks like that?" Mabel grumbled from above.

"It became my business when my mom texted me at

swim practice to tell me your mom is 'concerned' about you." Sam's air quotes were totally wasted on his absent audience.

"Why would she text you?"

"Because they know we're friends." And because his mom knew and Aunt Penny probably suspected Sam harbored a bit of a crush on Mabel.

"Go away," Mabel repeated. "I'm done with boys."

"Then you're in luck, because I'm a man." Sam grinned.

She snorted. "Seventeen isn't a man yet, doofus."

His grin widened. "Seventeen and a half. I'll buy you ice cream and let you play your music on the way into town."

"Fine!" There was movement above, then Mabel's sneakered feet and denim-clad legs started down the ladder. Soon her auburn curls were eye-level and she had two more steps to go to the bottom. It wasn't that Mabel was short, though she was, Sam's growth spurt at fourteen hadn't stopped since. His size thirteen shoes hinted he'd eventually reach his dad's height of six foot five.

She hopped from the last rung, and her fingers immediately began flying over her phone. "I texted Mom I'm leaving. I'm in the mood for sad country western music, so be prepared."

"Ah, the breakup playlist. Maybe you should reassess your dating choices if you've accumulated enough songs to warrant their own playlist." He let her lead the way across the yard to his driveway.

"Don't judge me. No questions till I have a spoonful of rocky road in my mouth. Hey, why are you wearing your glasses?"

"The wallower's break-up ice cream of choice." He smirked when she scowled at him. "You were having an emotional crisis." He shrugged." I didn't take the time to put my contacts back in after practice."

"Well, you look like a nerd." She rounded the car and got in.

Sam rolled his eyes, wishing for the days when Mabel was more sweet than salty.

****

"I told you what Brett was like." Sam sipped his vanilla malt.

"He was different in the beginning. But I caught him flirting with Madison when I ran back to my locker to get my science book." Mabel carefully scraped the spoon down the double scoop, shaving away bite after bite as she talked. "I'm never gonna find someone."

"Dramatic much? You're fifteen. You've got two years of high school left then the rest of your life. What's the rush?"

"I want someone just for me. Ya know?"

Yeah. He knew.

"I want to be special to someone."

"You're special to me." Sam tentatively exposed his heart.

"I know. We're friends." She placed another bite on her tongue.

Sam pulled his heart back into his chest and locked it up. "Yep, friends. You're the little sister I never hope I have."

Mabel laughed. "Gee, thanks. The feeling's mutual. I wouldn't want a sister as ugly as you. Our parents are old. No more siblings for either of us." She was quiet for a bit, scraping the last of her treat out of the bottom.

8

"Remember when we used to play book?"

Sam smiled. Mabel got over this heartbreak quicker than the last few. "I remember you bossing me around when we played dress up."

"Remember the stories our parents used to make up about going into books?"

"Yes." Sam wondered where the conversation was headed.

"Remember the mystery story we did with the book from my mom's closet?"

"Mabes, I remember a lot of things. What's your point?"

"Well, Mom sat me down the other day and I thought, 'oh, no. Not *the talk*'. But it wasn't that. She told me all those stories were true for the most part and it's all some crazy family legacy, which should be over now, but she wanted to make sure I knew in case any weird stuff ever happened. She said it skipped generations, so I'd have to be sure to tell my daughter."

Sam blinked and pushed his horn-rimmed glasses up on his nose. "Say again?"

"Yep. She said it was all true, and get this, she had the box from the closet out. She said it was everything about the legacy and I should read it and let her know if I have any questions."

"Seriously? Was she pranking you?" Aunt Penny had never been much of a jokester, but maybe she was growing senile.

"Yep and nope." She popped her Ps.

"Do you believe her?"

"Do you remember either of our parents ever specifically saying those stories were made-up?"

Sam thought back, but the stories were so much a

9

part of his childhood they'd taken on a life of their own. They played like movies in his memory, and he couldn't remember a time when he actually sat on a lap and listened to them being told. "No, but we were little. Everything's kind of blended together in my head."

"Mine, too." She began tearing up her napkin and dropping the shreds into her empty bowl.

"Do you believe her?"

"I believe she believes it. Maybe she had some kind of lucid dream. I'll have to ask Dad if she ever smoked pot."

"Have you gone through the box yet?"

"No time. It's a bunch of old books, a computer printed family tree—which is cool—and a stack of letters in granny handwriting."

"Sounds interesting."

"You're such an academic. It sounds boring as heck. If I want to learn how to churn butter or sew my own clothes, I'll look it up on the internet." She scoffed, then a sunny smile spread across her face. "Thank you, Sam. I feel better. What am I going to do next year when you leave for college?"

"Try dating fewer losers." Or fewer guys altogether. "I'm just a text away. You can call me. Best friends, right?"

Mabel reached over and squeezed his hand. "Yeah. Best friends forever."

Chapter 1

Glutton for Punishment

I clenched my fist, willing myself not to knock, as I stood outside Mabel's apartment. How many more times would I put myself through it? Despite living in neighboring towns and our families being close, I'd managed to avoid spending quality time with the girl who'd locked me in the friend zone.

But I always came if she truly needed me, like now, when Axel Doucheman's broken her heart. I've picked up the pieces of her heart enough times, you'd think I would own a bigger part of it. I sighed. I'd already driven across town, and it wasn't like I had any big plans for spring break anyway. I let my fist fall against the door.

I heard movement from the other side, encouraged that it wasn't wild sobbing. The chains rattled and the deadbolt turned before the door swung open revealing the familiar red eyes and puffy cheeks of my best friend.

"Sam!" Mabel flung herself into my arms.

I tensed, then let myself return the embrace. "I brought rocky road." I lifted the plastic sack in my hand.

Mabel hiccupped as a sob escaped. "You're always there for meee…" Her words trailed off as she buried her face in my chest.

An apartment door opened down the hall.

"Come on, weepy," I said as I penguin-walked her

backwards through the door. "Go sit on the couch while I put this in your freezer."

She sat and pulled a blanket over her head. The coffee table and floor were littered with crumpled tissues. I shook my head. I would never understand how such a smart, vibrant, confident girl—woman could let herself get so torn up over guys that weren't good enough for her.

I'd given the topic more thought than was probably healthy. She had a great family. My Uncle Tripp was awesome and always there for his kids, so no daddy-abandonment issues there. The only reasonable explanation I could come up with was Mabel's hopeless romanticism. She was in love with being in love. When the losers showed their true colors or realized they couldn't live up to her expectations, they checked out.

I found bowls in the cabinet and scooped out rocky road for her and vanilla I'd gotten for myself and prepared myself for a long night. I carried the bowls to the living room. Not much had changed in her apartment since her move-in party the previous summer. A footlocker, a newer version of the one in the tree house, still sat under the window where I'd placed it. Pictures hung on the wall: some artsy pieces I knew Bertie had painted and family photos. A rush of emotion squeezed my heart when I saw a photo of the two of us from my high school graduation included in the display.

"What happened with Doucheman?" I asked as I settled beside her.

She sniffed. "Dorfman."

"Po-tay-toes, po-tah-toes. Has he gone the way of the dodo?"

"You're so weird." She scooted closer and leaned

against me. "No glasses today?"

"Not much anymore." Though I had them with me in case I ended up crashing on the sofa. "Quit changing the subject."

"We planned for me to go with him to Boise over spring break. But yesterday he said he felt like we were in different places and thought we should take a break."

I gritted my teeth. "That's not so bad. You don't want to rush in to meeting his parents." I'd met Doucheman once when she brought him home for Thanksgiving several months ago. I wasn't a fan.

"I've been told by three other guys that we should take a break, and every time what they mean is a breakup." She commenced on a renewed crying jag.

I leaned back so I could put an arm around her shoulders. I was made of sterner stuff than most men my age in that female tears didn't bother me. Well, Mabel's break-up tears didn't bother me, at least. I'd learned a long time ago they represented the cleansing of yet another loser from her life. It used to give me hope she'd finally realize best friends made the best partners. After living this exact scenario six or seven times, I learned Mabel would never see me as such without a grand gesture on my part. I wouldn't risk our friendship like that.

"Your sofa is a lot more comfortable for this than your tree house," I teased.

She grabbed the tissue box from the table and blew her nose. "We had some good times up there, though."

"Yeah, we did, before you became a teenage watering pot."

She smacked my chest, a good sign the worst was coming to an end. "You had your share of tears up there."

"Never!" I laughed. If she only knew how I'd pined for her.

"Remember when we used to play book?"

"Sure. It was all we ever did. Turned me into an avid reader, though."

"I think Aunt Bobbie did that." Mabel laughed. "I finally got around to looking through that box."

"What box?"

"Remember when I told you my mom said all the stories were real? There's a gypsy curse and a family legacy. It's how my parents met."

"You didn't tell me that. You said it was boring books and old lady letters and you thought your mom had a psychotic break." I reluctantly lifted her off me so I could see her face.

"I finally got around to reading everything. It's a pretty elaborate hoax if it's not real. Your mom told you stories, too. There was a whole notebook full of magic rules that she wrote."

"Really?" My mom was not what you'd consider fanciful.

"Yeah. All the books were the ones my ancestresses had 'read' into. That's what our moms called it, 'reading-in' to the stories. They would read and then they'd literally be in the story. There was a family tree all the way back to the 1700s for both my mom and my dad and letters, really old ones, that all backed up what Mom said."

Mabel spoke the truth, or at least she believed what she told me. Gypsy magic wasn't real. "Where is all this stuff?" I needed hard evidence.

"Mom still has it."

I grabbed a paperback from underneath a pile of

tissues. "You're saying, if you open this and start reading, we'll both magically be in the story? Where's this guy's shirt anyway?"

"Give me that!" She made a grab for it, but I held it out of reach.

"*Love's Gamble*. Will Rose take a gamble on love? Ooh." I made immature kissing noises. "Answer the question, Mabes."

She crossed her arms. "No. I'd end up in the story with my true love."

Ouch. "Of course."

"It doesn't work anymore, anyway. Mom found my dad and he is the descendant of my great, great, great, great grandmother Elizabeth's destined true love."

My arm slackened. "Your parents are related?"

Mabel made another swipe at the book, so I raised it again. "No, pay attention. Elizabeth didn't marry her destined true love. She married a gypsy man." She expelled a breath. "It's a long story. Give me my book back and I'll explain."

"Maybe you have so many man troubles because you read this garbage. It gives you unrealistic expectations."

She rolled her eyes. "Quit being a brat."

"What's it even about? He's wearing a cowboy hat. I think cowboys usually wear shirts, especially back in the days when women wore dresses like that. Hers appears to be missing a few buttons, though."

"Sam…" I ignored her warning tone. "I don't know what it's about; I'm not very far."

"Well, let's see. I opened it with one hand to the page with the dog-eared corner. "Chapter two. That's pretty far."

"Fine. The heroine is trying to save her ranch after her parents died. There's a slimy dude trying to woo it away from her."

"Ah ha! Enter the hero, sans shirt," I teased. "Ah hem. Clifton McGrath dragged himself across the barren landscape…"

Love's Gamble

…he hoped his faithful steed, Bolt, would find his way back to Cliff eventually. He was a smart horse, but even the best mount will spook at the sight of a rattler in its path.

Left with nothing but the shirt on his back and his pistol, he was soon relieved of those as well by a band of thieves. Took his boots, too. Cliff was in a right sorry way. When a dilapidated ranch house appeared in the distance, his poor luck led him to believe it was nothing but a mirage. Two days without water would do that to a man.

The creak of the windmill and dresses flapping on the clothesline made for a mighty detailed mirage. The barking mutt that ran out to scare him off finally convinced him of its reality.

He smoothed back his dark brown hair and wiped a hand down his face, embarrassed to encounter a week's growth of stubble. There would be no improving his appearance. He'd just have to depend on the rancher's Christian character and generous disposition.

The dog ceased barking and followed close at Cliff's heels as he climbed the steps to the porch. He clenched his fist, regretting the circumstances leading him to this point, and let it rap against the roughhewn door.

He glanced at his surroundings while he waited. He would offer to work in exchange for food, water, a bath, and a shirt. It looked like an older couple hadn't been able to keep up with the day to day needs of a working ranch, or perhaps the hands were slacking. He'd be glad to help for a few days while he recovered and reclaimed his bearings.

The door opened. Cliff spun back to greet not a bent old man, but a young woman with wild auburn hair and fire in her eyes to match.

"Damn it, Sam. What have you done?"

Chapter 2

Spoke Too Soon
Love's Gamble

A shocked expression crossed my visitor's face and he stammered, "I, I need to see the man of the house please, ma'am."

"Knock it off, Sam." I snapped my fingers in his face. I did not have time for Sam's amnesia. Everything my mother said proved to be true—except for the part about the legacy being finished with her marriage to my dad.

Sam was an English Lit major. I needed every resource available to help me figure this out. Plus, I was terrified; I needed my friend, not this grungy, shirtless cowboy.

Sam cocked his head. "Ma'am?"

I grabbed his shoulders, giving him a shake. "You're Samuel Earvin Celansky. I'm nobody's ma'am. It's me, Mabel Elizabeth Kinney, your best friend."

Sam blinked several times, then his eyes widened. He stepped back and turned full around before his gaze found me again. He took in my calico dress and the apron tied at my waist before his eyes found mine again. "Mabes? Where in the hell are we and where is my shirt?"

I grinned. There's my Sam. "Close your eyes." He

did. "Think back to when you were walking up to the door."

He took a deep breath. "I'm dirty and hungry and I need help."

"Good. Now remember farther back." Crow's feet formed as he squeezed his eyes shut tighter. "I lost my horse. No, a snake spooked him. Thieves stole my gun, boots, and shirt." He opened his eyes. "What's going on?"

I smiled. "It looks like we're not too old to play book after all."

****

"Damn it, Sam! When I wished men would fall at my feet, I didn't mean you." At least he'd had the good manners to faint over the threshold, so I didn't have to drag him so far. He had an unusually large amount of muscle for an academic. Not that I noticed on purpose. When he fell into me, all I could do was keep him from hitting the ground quite so fast. All that muscle was heavy.

I took a closer look at my home's interior. Not much furniture to speak of and certainly no sofa. The floor, then. I heaved him face-up and placed a folded blanket under his head, noticing the differences between book Sam and real Sam.

I brushed the longer hair away from his forehead. His face needed washing and a shave. His mustache was full-grown, probably what the character usually wore, but the beard was new growth and not manscaped. All together it made my Sam look older and more worldly. Not to mention the un-Sam-like tattoo I'd glimpsed on his shoulder when I'd pulled him inside. His lashes fluttered.

"Ma'am?"

"Ugh. Not again. Sam, it's me, Mabel."

"Mabel?" He attempted to sit.

"Hold your horses there, Tex. I can't have you checking out on me again. I need your expertise."

Sam glanced around the sparse room. "I'm not an expert on anything here."

"Books and reading. We're in a book."

He shifted up on his elbows. "Based on our last conversation, this has more to do with your family than anything I've read. Are we in that book? The one with the shirtless cowboy?"

I grinned. "It looks like. Guess what, you're the shirtless cowboy."

Sam looked down at his chest. "Shit," he muttered. "Where's my shirt?"

"Stolen by thieves, remember?"

He met my gaze. "Oddly, yeah. I do remember. I got the crap beat out of me after being thrown off my horse." He sat up fully, twisting at the waist. I accidentally watched the muscles in his arms as they flexed and bulged. "My sore muscles don't feel fictional. Is that how it's supposed to work?"

"According to the notes, yes. But nothing permanent can happen to you, like death."

"Good to know. So, what happens next? Please tell me it involves a bath." He scratched at his beard.

Warmth crept up my face as I thought of the mechanics involved in getting Sam a bath. I knew there was no bathroom or shower. That meant a washtub behind a thin curtain. He'd need a bar of lye soap and someone to wash his hair. Crap! Maybe I did read too many sexy romance novels. "Um…let me look outside for a washtub."

Outside the backdoor, an oval galvanized tin washtub leaned against the house. I manhandled it through the door and dragged it toward the only bedroom.

"Hey. I'll get that." Sam rolled over to push himself up.

I dropped the tub and hurried over. "Hold on, let me help you." He didn't need my help, so I served as more of a spotter. "I'm just going to drag it a few more feet into the bedroom so you can have some privacy."

He took a few steps and stopped. "I don't think you are, actually."

The stupid tub was filled to the brim with water and a bar of soap sat in a tray hooked to the side.

"Wha—how did that happen?"

Sam smirked. "Looks like the magic is more interested in my being clean than having privacy."

"Ha! Well, I'll just sit in the bedroom while you wash."

"Do you think there's a shirt for me somewhere and maybe shoes and a razor?" Sam moved to the tub and tested the water. "At least it's warm."

"And we didn't have to lug it. I'll check. If this was my character's parents' home, presumably my father will still have clothes here." A double bed sat against the wall next to the door, spread with a colorful, but faded patchwork quilt. A simple wooden chest of drawers sat on the opposite wall.

A small, open box on top the chest held a shaving kit: soap cup, brush, straight razor, and folded strop. I opened the blade with care. It appeared in good shape to my untrained eye. Maybe Sam would be able to tell.

I tried the drawers. The top two held women's clothes, undergarments, and more calico dresses. The third held men's pants, shirts, and long underwear. No fruits of the loom, here. I snickered. The bottom drawer held folded pieces of flannel. I pulled one out and shook it open. It was about bath towel size. Duh. Terrycloth probably hadn't been invented or was considered a luxury. The flannel *was* a bath towel.

I draped it over my arm along with a set of the man's clothes. Grabbing the shaving kit, I went back into the other room. "Sam, I f…" Sam's naked back greeted me.

I spun away, but not before noticing again the muscle definition in my friend's back as he sat in the tub and bent to dunk his head. The water sloshed and Sam inhaled. "What are you doing? Why are you naked already?"

"I couldn't wait. You were occupied; I figured it was a good time to get in. What's the problem? You've seen me naked before." A smirk laced his voice.

"Not for about twenty years!"

"Mmm, closer to fifteen. Remember that time we went camping?"

I stomped my foot. I felt at a disadvantage not being able to see his face. "We were children. I sure don't want to see you naked now." *Though I'd love to get a closer look at his ink.*

"Then don't turn around." His voice hardened, as if I'd offended him.

"Here." I thrust the shaving kit behind me. "I can't tell is it's sharp or not, but there's a strop thingy."

Sam lifted the kit from my hand. "I know you said we can't die, but you also said the legacy was over. I'm not going to risk accidentally slitting my own throat.

Thanks, though." He set it on the floor. "What else did you find?"

"Clothes, but the pants look short. The shirt should be fine. Do you want the long johns for underwear?" Heat crept up my neck.

Sam chuckled. "Apparently this cowboy goes commando. All I had on was pants and socks, but those are trash after walking in them. Did you find boots?"

Now my cheeks burned as well. "I'll check." Keeping my back to the tub, I shuffled to the dining table and dragged one of the wooden chairs within arms' reach of Sam. "Here's the clothes. You can use this big piece of fabric for a towel." I set everything on the chair.

"Thank you." Joking aside, Sam's tone was sincere.

"Of course. It's my fault we're here. I'll just go in the bedroom till you're done."

"Mabel?"

I paused.

"Would you mind taking the pants I had on and beating them against the outside of the house or something? If you don't think the pants you found will fit me, you're probably right. I can just wear the old ones."

"Sure!" I said more brightly than I felt. I picked the pants up off the floor and carried them outside, trying not to think about how recently they'd been wrapped around naked Sam.

Chapter 3

Cue the Villain's Theme
Love's Gamble

The sound of Mabel ruthlessly beating my pants against the porch rail made me glad I wasn't in them. Once she finished exercising her stress and I was clothed, maybe we could figure a way out of this predicament. I'd have to find out more details about this legacy thing.

I made quick work of soaping my hair, beard, and body, the lye soap tightening my skin as badly as the pool at the gym. The mustache would take some getting used to. I'd never worn one—I glanced down. Sure enough, my usually meticulously shaved chest now sprouted a healthy patch of curling dark hairs. "The guy on the cover didn't have chest hair," I grumbled. I wasn't a fanatic about shaving, I mean, I didn't bother with my legs or anything, but I'd challenged myself to cut a whole second off my 100-freestyle time. Keeping drag to a minimum was part of my strategy.

I rose from the tub and sluiced most of the water off my skin, keeping a wary eye on the door. I wrapped the flannel around my waist and tucked the tail. Next, I held the pants up to my body. Not only were they too short, they'd almost fit two of me. Mabel must have forgotten the shirt, so I sat in the chair and pulled on the socks.

The front door burst open, and my pants hit me in

the face.

"Quick, get dressed. There's someone coming up the driveway," Mabel hissed.

I stood. "You forgot the shirt and I still need boots."

She came over and spun me toward the bedroom. Hands touched my back then flew away as if burned before settling again and giving me a solid push. "Hurry up. I don't know if I'll need you in this scene or not. Your mom always used to read ahead so my mom would at least have some idea what would happen. Just listen from in here until I figure out if this is the bad guy or my love interest." With one last shove she removed her hands and pulled the door nearly closed.

I pulled on my pants and found a shirt in a wooden dresser. Boots? I scanned the sparse room. Maybe her father was buried in them. I bent and flipped the edge of the quilt. Under the bed sat a pair of worn square-toe cowboy boots and, to my relief, a shotgun and box of shells.

The boots fit as well as someone else's boots could be expected to fit, but at least they didn't pinch. I pulled out the rifle and shells and set them on the bed. Would I be expected to shoot someone? Thanks to Mabel's dad, I was a pretty fair shot with a variety of firearms. I froze, stunned.

Mabel could shoot, too. We could both throw axes, fence, and use recurve and crossbows. Her dad set up a range in the backyard. I thought he was just into weapons. For the first time I wondered if perhaps he had another purpose for trying to turn all us kids into little warriors.

"Well, howdy do, stranger. What brings you out to this next of the woods?" Mabel affected a ridiculous southern drawl to answer the door as Rose.

I pulled on the boots and crept to the bedroom door. Peering through the crack, I could see Rose's back. She didn't open the door all the way, so I couldn't make out the visitor.

"Miss Rose, do you mind if I address you as such?"

Mabel giggled. Probably because she couldn't even remember her character's last name.

"Rose, I came to see if you'd like to step out with me, perhaps go for a walk," the jerk said, dropping the *Miss* altogether.

I slotted him as the frontrunner for the bad guy position. Hadn't Mabel said someone was trying to buy Rose's land? I glanced at the gun still on the bed. I leaned over and grabbed it. I was glad to find it loaded, though I only planned to use it as a threat. I turned my attention back to the front of the house.

"…good time. I have so much to do. Maybe another day," Mabel said.

The man stepped into view and took Mabel's hand. "I really must insist. You wouldn't be so busy if you took a husband to help you with the ranch. It's just too much for a lone woman."

Mabel attempted to free her hand, but the man held fast.

Time to intercede. I stepped out of the bedroom, making sure each fall of my boots sounded ominous. I got my first good look at the unwanted visitor.

I supposed he wasn't bad looking. He had longish blond hair and a mustache. Dark brown eyes that appeared a bit beady, truth be told. His clothes were too slick and clean, like he'd never performed an honest day's work. Definitely the story's antagonist. I cocked the shotgun.

"Who're you?" he asked, dropping Mabel's hand.

"I'm a friend of the family," I answered, trying to match the man's glare. Confrontation was not part of my normal life.

The man snorted. "I ain't never heard of no other kin, least of all a cousin."

Huh?

Mabel spoke out the side of her mouth. "I read about this. He's a scripted character. Your character must introduce himself as a cousin in the book."

Keeping my eyes on the immediate threat, I responded in kind. "Am I your cousin?"

"I have no idea. I only read chapter one, remember," she hissed.

"Well, I've never heard of you so that makes us even steven. Mab—Rose said she's busy today and all the rest of the days, so you can just take off." I raised the gun slightly.

Mabel smacked my arm. "Sam! Don't run him off completely. What if he's my love interest?"

"He's not. He was being disrespectful."

"Maybe you're the bad guy and he's supposed to run you off?" She put her hands on her hips in a classic 'obstinate Mabel' stance I was quite familiar with.

"You said it was all scripted. I guess we'll find out soon enough." It was a bit odd having a conversation in front of someone who seemed completely oblivious.

"I'll be back, fragile Rose. And you'll regret not taking me up on my offer to do this the easy way." He spun on his heel and stomped back to his horse, a big black stallion, of course.

"What a dick." Mabel brushed past me as she

entered the house.

I followed. Using a falsetto voice, I said, "OMG, Sam. You were right. That guy was totally the villain."

She turned and narrowed her eyes at me.

I bit back a grin and cleared my throat. "So what now?"

"The scene is over. I guess we just wait to get sent home. I'll call my mom when we get back and see if she knows what's going on. She was sure the legacy was over. Not only that, the magic was only triggered at the death of a grandmother."

"But in order for a woman to be a grandmother, there has to be a granddaughter. So it stand to reason that the legacy doesn't pass to a daughter because the daughter is already married. All of the women died when they were old," I said, working it out in my head as I spoke. Maybe I should have kept it to myself.

Mabel paled. "Do you think something happened to my mother?"

"No! Geez, no." I pulled Mabel into my arms, cursing my loose lips. "Something else is happening here. Your mom is fine, I'm sure of it." I wracked my brain trying to come up with something to support my statement. "Let's just sit at the table and wait to go home."

Mabel sniffed and nodded her head against my shirt. "It should be any time."

Chapter 4

To Market, to Market
Love's Gamble

Three hours later I wanted to scream. Sam and I had played dozens of games of checkers with an antique set I found in a cabinet and concerns about my mom's well-being continued to haunt me. Sam did his best to distract me by pumping me for every last bit of information I knew about the legacy.

My stomach emitted a vicious growl.

Sam smirked. "Hungry?"

"Aren't you? We've been here forever. Something isn't right. My mom—"

"Stop. You can't change anything by worrying about it. Not a damn thing. You're just going to stress yourself out and delay us getting out of this situation. If we haven't gone back, it must mean there's something more we have to do first." Sam scooped up the checkers and returned them to the little burlap baggie.

He was right. I needed to think rationally. We already knew the legacy wasn't proceeding in the normal way. My mom wasn't dead. She wasn't! And I hadn't met my true love yet. The bad guy, Jake, or something, couldn't be it. He wasn't the hero. Unless the magic made changes to that rule, too. "The first scene is obviously over. We need to figure out what comes next."

"Let's start with dinner." Sam rose and started opening bins and cabinets.

"I'm not a great cook to begin with. Unless you find a package of pasta and a jar of sauce, I won't be much help." I started searching on the other side of the small kitchen area. We combined our findings on the table. "Cornmeal, dry beans, one egg, a block of yeast, and a tin of salt. I'm out. I can't do anything with this."

Sam scratched the back of his head. "Yeah. One egg won't be enough for both of us. Beans have to soak overnight, or they'll be crunchy. I learned that the hard way at a scout camp out."

"Maybe we should go into town? We have to learn information from other characters to move the story forward. I found a tin with some coins. We can buy more ingredients to actually make something or eat dinner in town."

"Or buy a cookbook. No Google here, or cell service, for that matter," Sam added.

As I emptied the coin tin into my pocket, horses whinnied outside.

Looking out the window, Sam said, "We must be on the right track. Your wagon is out front with two horses hitched to it. And I think my wayward horse found me."

I hurried out the front door. My dog was asleep on the porch, I'd wondered what happened to it, and the horses were waiting to take us to town. It looked like I'd have to drive myself as Sam rode for whatever reason.

Sam stepped onto the porch behind me holding the shotgun. "I'm taking this with us. It can go in the wagon under a blanket or something, but I'd feel better having it."

"Fine by me."

He walked over to his horse and greeted it with pats and soft words. My heart felt a little squishy for some reason. Dumb. Sam had always been kind to animals. Why would fictional animals be any different. His horse nuzzled Sam's shirt, then sneezed.

"Ah! Gross. Let me get a new shirt then we can leave." He came toward me unbuttoning his snotty shirt.

That reminded me. "Hey, just in case it comes up later in the story for whatever reason, you should know your character has a tattoo on his upper back."

Sam paused, shirt halfway undone, and his cheeks colored. "It's mine."

"What? You don't have any tattoos. Let me see." I helped him with the rest of his buttons. His flush had spread to his neck and chest.

He peeled the shirt off and I stepped around him so I could inspect his back. His muscley back. The basic black tattoo was about the size of my palm and covered a portion of his left shoulder. It featured an open book with trees, a mountain, a river, and random swirls growing up from the pages. Above the book, a ribbon with words read 'My Passion' and below, one said 'My Downfall'.

"Sam, it's beautiful and depressing all at the same time."

"Thanks. I think. I'll go get that shirt." He started to walk away.

"Wait." I traced my finger over the design and Sam shivered. "What does it mean?"

He shrugged. "Nothing. I heard it somewhere and liked it. I like books and sometimes spend too much time reading." Goosebumps rose on his skin.

"Dramatic much? It's called procrastination.

Everyone does it." I couldn't help myself. I ran my nail down the indent of his spine, and he shivered again. "You're cold. Hurry and get your shirt."

****

"So that's how a scene change works!" Sam and I were on the road towards town. I could only assume we headed in the right direction; the horses just did their preprogrammed thing. When we started out, there was nothing but ranch land as far as the eye could see. After about five minutes, the town appeared about a mile in the distance like a mirage. I turned around on my seat to see how far we'd come from the house. Nothing. The ranch was nowhere in sight. It was a bit disconcerting, but, I supposed, having characters spending hours and hours traveling didn't serve the plot.

Sam turned to look, too. "Interesting. It must be how the magic works with the plot to eliminate dead space. Nothing of import happens on the way to town, therefore it doesn't have to take the hour or however long it's supposed to."

My stomach rumbled again. "Thank goodness for that. Let's find a fast-food restaurant."

Sam opened his mouth to speak.

"Kidding! I'm not an idiot. We'll find the store."

"Mercantile," Sam mumbled.

"Whatever." I turned to face forward again, though my gaze wanted to linger on cowboy Sam. He rode proficiently. Not as well as me, but pretty good. He sat relaxed in the saddle, his hips swaying with the horse's gait. I should have insisted I ride, and he drive the wagon, but after I'd teased him about his tattoo, I was feeling a bit contrite.

From our vantage point, the town appeared to

consist of one long street, adjacent to the one on which we approached. It sat smack in the middle of daggum nowhere. The roads leading out of either end petered away into the landscape. Creepy. When we arrived, our side street met the main road between a laundry and a dress shop. My horses turned left but Sam's mount veered to the right.

I turned to yell. "Hey! Where are you going?"

Holding both hands in the air, he called over his shoulder, "Wherever the story takes me. Whoever finds food, bring some back to share." The town's hustle and bustle swallowed him up.

There were people and horses and wagons everywhere. A stagecoach was parked across the street, making me laugh. Where did people take the stage to, from one end of town to the other? Maybe once it hit the edge of town it simply disappeared, having no further part in the story.

Thankfully, the townsfolk seemed to part like the Red Sea for my wagon. No steering required. The horses pulled up outside a large building with a sign reading Bluebonnet Grange Hall. Ah. I'd forgotten the book was set in Texas.

Though the sun had been high in the sky moments ago, it now kissed the horizon and town noise decreased. My horses pulled me into a lot next to the grange and I was joined by more wagons and men on horseback. A few tipped their hats in greeting and a young woman waved a hello before going inside the building. The mood was festive.

"I guess I'm going to a party. At least there'll be food." I set the brake on the wagon (I'd seen Little House enough times to know to do that) and had a word with the horses. "You two stay put. I don't have anything to tie you to."

Music and light filtered out of the grange as I followed a family up the stairs. Once inside they headed off to greet friends, leaving me with my first unobstructed view of the party.

Hay bales formed a large square in the middle of the room to designate a dance area. To my left, people visited at tables covered with red and white checked cloths. Directly across from me, on the other side of the dance floor, men served drinks from tapped barrels. A little boy left the area carrying two full mugs, so I sincerely hoped the barrels held cider and not beer.

To my left, long covered tables were piled high with breads, cookies, and pies. Score! That was my first stop. I headed that direction, sidestepping a woman intent on chatting me up. A glance back witnessed her gossiping with the empty space where I had stood. I laughed, but it reminded me to keep my eyes open for my true love. This would be the ideal place to meet him.

I turned back to my destination. Several older women in calico were cutting pies and serving food. A pair of hands caught my attention. Familiar fingers drummed the table and the distinctive wedding set glinted in the lantern light. My gaze followed the calico-clad arm up to equally familiar curly auburn hair, well on its way to escaping its bun.

"Mom?"

Chapter 5

Support Your Local Law Enforcement
Love's Gamble
Though I hated letting Mabel out of my sight, I trusted her faith in the legacy magic. Besides, I needed to give my emotions a reality check. The abbreviated ride to town did not give me enough time to recover from the feeling of Mabel's fingers on my bare skin.

My explanation of the ink's meaning had been lame, at best. Mabel could never know the artwork was the product of too much alcohol and a pity party. She was, is my passion. If I can't let her go, she'll be my downfall. Being stuck here with her while she seeks out the man she'll marry will be torture, but it's the cruel wake-up call I need to finally move on. *Thanks, legacy. You suck.*

My horse parked itself in front of the sheriff's office. I'd go in, report Mabel's unwanted visitor, and see what I could learn.

The man behind the desk rose as I entered the office. "Evenin', Ranger. What brings you by our little town?"

I glanced over my shoulder. No one there. He was talking to me. "Uh. To be honest, I don't rightly know. I'm hoping you can help me out." I stuck out my hand to grasp his. Something jabbed me in my left thigh. I stuck my hand in my pocket and pulled out a shiny Texas Ranger badge. Huh. I couldn't believe it survived the beating Mabel gave my pants. I pinned it on my chest.

This guy was not a grizzled old sheriff. I scratched my beard. No, this man knew how to use a straight razor and had probably been clean-shaven this morning. The five o'clock shadow he now wore did nothing to hide his ridiculously chiseled cheekbones and stupid cleft chin. He had 'true love' written all over him. Not that I was jealous. I needed to remember that while he was the sheriff here in the book, he was also a real person somewhere in the real world. Probably a model or fireman. Great.

"I'm Sheriff Beau Wilson. Seems I have heard that name. Let me take a look." He picked up a pile of papers from his desk. He pulled a wanted poster from the pile and handed it to me. "Jace Cutter. This came on yesterday's stage. Can't say I've seen the man yet. You say he's in town?"

"Uh, yes. He's harassing Mab—Rose. Trying to force her to sell her land." I took the paper. The likeness was pretty good, but only because I'd seen the man in real life. I don't know that I'd be able to pick Jace Cutter out of a crowd based on this police sketch. Cutter appeared to be an all-around bad guy. The list included forgery, theft, impersonation of government land officials, gambling cons, and counterfeiting.

Sheriff Beau got a vacant look in his eyes. "Ah, sweet Rose. Such a shame about her folks. She should have come to me if that fella was giving her trouble."

I frowned. "That's what I'm doing now. She had some errands to run."

He brightened. "I imagine most of the town is there. In fact, I was fixin' to head that way myself."

"On errands?" I suspect this was just the beginning

of weird conversations with townsfolk.

"Come on. I'll walk with you to the Grange Hall. The harvest dance should be just beginning. Rose is probably savin' a dance for me. I told her I'd meet her."

Ah. "Lead on."

****

"Mom!" I hurried across the hall, relief flooding me. She met me halfway, and we fell into each other's arms. "I'm so glad you're alive."

"Mabel! I wondered how we got here." She held up her hand with her grandmother's wedding ring and wiggled her fingers. "The magic must be up to its old tricks. I'm sorry, sweetie. I didn't think it would actually happen to you, but I am alive and well."

My dad joined us carrying two mugs. "It was either beer or cider, and I figured we'd better keep our wits about us." He turned and gave me a one-armed hug after handing off one of the mugs. "Hi, sweetheart. First time?"

"I thought you said the magic was satisfied."

Mom cocked an eyebrow at me. "If you read all the notes, you'd remember that the magic is also persnickety."

"Read as 'asspain,'" my dad said, sipping his cider.

"I need to know how to find my true love so I can go home. I assume that's why I'm here."

Mom glanced around the hall. "Did you just arrive? He should be here any minute."

I folded my arms over my waist. "I've been here forever! So many scenes! That's not how it's supposed to go, according to all the notes."

"This is already an unusual situation since your dad and I are here. Tell me who you met in the first scene."

"I started the book last week, so this is chapter two, I think. We might be further than that now. The only person I've met is the villain. Could it be him?"

Mom tilted her head in thought. "I suppose it's possible, if his character is later redeemed somehow. Tell me what happened."

"Well, Sam and I—"

Dad cut in. "Sam's here?"

I sighed. "Axel dumped me."

"Dorkman? Good. He wasn't good enough for my little girl." Dad gave me another warm squeeze.

I rolled my eyes. "Anyway, Sam was at my apartment and now we're both here." I looked at Mom. "Your notes said it's how Aunt Bobbie came with you. Proximity."

"It was indeed." A strange look passed between my parents.

I continued with my story. "Sam dragged himself to my front door and I doctored him up." I left out all the naked bits. They weren't relevant to the story. "Then the villain rode up and harassed me about my land. Sam ran him off with a shotgun. We waited for a scene change that never came, got hungry, and the horses appeared out front and took us to town. We split up when we got here. Which reminds me. I need some of that pie."

"Interesting." Dad nodded. "Where's Sam now?"

Chapter 6

Do Si Do
Love's Gamble

I followed Sheriff Beau into the Grange Hall, squinting against the sudden brightness. A band of sorts was set up next to a makeshift dance floor. They resembled an old-timey tinker's wagon as much as a musical group. Two men played fiddles; a woman slapped spoons against her thigh while a grizzled old man ran a stick down a washboard. Another man ran a bow across a saw. They sounded pretty good, surprisingly.

In my peripheral, I noticed the sheriff wander off. A young woman in braids placed a plate with pie and a fork in my hands. My stomach grumbled. Perfect timing. I shoveled in bites as I surveyed the room.

Couples twirled around the dance floor, bouncing in time to the music. I picked out a head of auburn curls somewhere in the middle, and my heart jumped. Seconds later, the couple circled around to the edge. Uncle Tripp led Aunt Penny across the floor in a lively reel. I didn't even know he could dance. Relief at my aunt's proof of life battled with surprise at Uncle Tripp's newfound dexterity.

My gaze followed the couple until the crowd absorbed them and it snagged on a second auburn head.

Mabel stood off to the side, clapping in time to the music. Lamplight glinted off her curls, and a smile lit her face as she watched her parents circle the floor. A hand touched her shoulder.

Sheriff Beau. Mabel turned, and her face brightened even more. I shouldn't interfere, let the magic work its, well, magic. But there was no reason I couldn't vet this joker like I would any other guy. I stalked over.

"Sam!" Mabel's delight was laced with panic. "Have you met the sheriff?" She leaned toward me and whispered, "I don't know what he's talking about."

"Sheriff Beau Wilson," I said with a twang. "I walked over with him from the police station, er, sheriff's office. He's just in character. It takes some getting used to. He won't notice you're not following along." In fact, Beau continued to ramble the entire time Mabel talked to me.

"I think he might be the one." She glanced back at the sheriff.

"Really?" I feigned surprise. "What makes you think that?"

"Duh. He's the best-looking guy here." Her eyes flicked to mine, then quickly away as she spoke.

Though I agreed, I wouldn't make it easy for her. "Way to judge a cover, Mabes. He's probably not a do-gooder sheriff in the real world. What if he's a criminal?"

She huffed and crossed her arms. "The magic wouldn't do that to me."

I released a little of my tightly held frustration. "You have no idea what the magic will or will not do. It brought us here and abandoned us. You may get true love out of it, but apparently, I'm just along for the ride."

"The magic has always worked for the good of the

women in my family. Even though things are happening a little differently now, I don't have any reason to believe that's changed. Look at my dad." She gestured toward the dance floor. "I've never seen him dance like that before. In the books, he has his leg back. That's why it took my parents three books to get together." She sniffed and wiped at her eyes.

I looked back at the dance floor. My uncle lowered his wife into a deep dip before two-stepping away again. Uncle Tripp didn't let his prosthetic leg keep him from living a normal life, but he walked with a slight hitch in his step and avoided activities where his disability might be a hindrance…like fast dancing.

The sheriff placed a hand on Mabel's elbow and steered her toward the dance floor. She started to protest.

"You'd better go with him. Otherwise, he'll just end up circling the floor by himself." I wouldn't mind seeing that, but I was there to support Mabel.

She frowned but allowed herself to be herded. I searched her face every time she passed where I stood. Her expression varied between amused and confused, but, to my satisfaction, never appeared enthralled or love stuck.

A creamy pale hand brushed my sleeve. "It's not often we get a real live Texas Ranger 'round these parts."

I glanced at my badge, having forgotten its presence. Mabel hadn't even mentioned it. *Thanks, Magic.* I needed one more reminder of how little attention my crush paid me. "You want to dance?" I interrupted the blushing Texas flower mid-sentence. She stared at me blankly. It looked like we were going off-script. I grasped her elbow and propelled her to the dance floor.

As the dance steps I'd learned years ago slowly

came back to me, a new thought occurred. While Uncle Tripp and my dad insisted their children learned all the ways of weaponry and the outdoors, my mom and Aunt Penny dragged us to dance lessons, museums, and historical reenactments. The six of us, me, my brother, Mabel and Bertie, and their two cousins, were the most learned, well-rounded kids you'd ever want to meet or survive a zombie apocalypse with.

My partner kept pace with my steps but had given up on conversation, thank goodness. Uncle Tripp and Aunt Penny noticed me and waved, ridiculous grins plastered on their faces. I hoped I'd have a chance to chat with them later. The song ended and the sheriff escorted Mabel off the dance floor. I maneuvered in their direction.

I thanked the girl for the dance and headed toward Mabel in time to see another man escort her to the floor. This time, I ignored the young misses who approached. Guilt beat at me, but they were just characters. It wasn't like I snubbed real girls with real feelings. Sheriff Beau returned with a mug of cider.

"She's dancing again," I told him, tilting my head at the dancers.

Beau nodded. "I do. I care for her very much. I'm trying to wait a respectable amount of time before I begin courting in earnest. Her parents haven't been gone but six months."

I didn't know if I'd ever get used to talking to someone with scripted dialogue. Beau obviously responded to a question asked by Cliff about his and Rose's relationship. According to what Mabel had explained, the next step was getting this clown to self-evolve or self-realize or something like that. She said it might take a traumatic incident, but her dad had been able to speak off-script before he became aware. I could try that.

"So, Sheriff, did you always want to be in law enforcement?"

"Her pa and mine were friends. I'm a few years older, but I've known Rose all her life." He stared wistfully at Mabel as she danced by.

Maybe I should try a different line of questioning. "Who do you like for president in the coming election, Lincoln, Kennedy, or Reagan?"

"If things go as planned, I'll make her an offer at Christmas. Though, I don't care for her being alone way out there on the ranch." Beau frowned.

Fine. I'd play the game. "No need to fear, my good man. Since my quarry seems so interested in her property, I thought I'd hang out there in case he comes round again."

Beau narrowed his eyes at me, assessing. "Much obliged."

Mabel's partner deposited her next to us. She lifted the cider from Beau's hand. "For me? What a sweetie."

"Ranger McGrath tells me you're puttin' him up at your place. You all right with that arrangement? I can post deputies if you want, and the ranger can stay in town." The sheriff angled his body to nudge me out of the conversation.

Mabel peeked at me over his shoulder. "Ranger?" Her gaze landed on my badge. "Oh! Yes, of course. I'm perfectly safe with the ranger. I wouldn't dream of taking your deputies away from their duties."

Beau offered her his arm. "Care for another turn?"

Mabel handed me her cider and took his arm. "Why

not?"

I closed my hand around her arm. "Why not? It won't hurt twinkle toes to take a turn by himself while you stay here and tell me what you learned from your parents."

She sighed, but patted Beau's arm and gave him a little shove toward the dance floor. He smiled and escorted empty air away from them, none the wiser. Tempting as it was to watch the sheriff make a fool of himself, I focused my attention on Mabel.

"So, what did they say?"

"Not much. They're as mystified as I am but are taking advantage of their time here."

"I noticed. I'm glad for them, but it doesn't help us. Do we just hang out until the end of the book?" I frowned. Watching Mabel fall in love didn't sound like anything I wanted to hang around for.

"There'll probably be some rescuing. You're a ranger, so you probably have an important part, too. Maybe you get to apprehend the bad guy while Beau rescues me." Mabel tapped her chin in thought.

"You don't sound very disturbed about being kidnapped."

"I can't really get hurt in the book."

"Says who?" I scowled.

She planted her hands on her hips. "Says the magic."

"You say that like it hasn't been behaving peculiarly thus far."

Mabel smirked. "You always start using high-dollar words when you get agitated."

"Can you please take this seriously?"

"Fine." She retrieved the cider I'd been holding and took a sip. She held up the mug to offer me some.

As I shook my head to decline, Mabel lurched forward, drenching me with the mug's contents. The man who'd knocked into her kept walking without acknowledging his misstep.

"Hey!"

Mabel placed her hand on my chest. "Shh. It doesn't matter. We were probably just in the way of his scripted action." She pulled her hand away from my soaking shirt. "I didn't realize there was that much cider left in the cup. I'm sorry, Sam."

The only part of my shirt not dripping was the back. It made no sense.

She placed the mug on the floor. "Here, let me have it so you can find somewhere to clean up. You're not going to want to bother with another bath once we get back to the house." Her gaze bounced around, landing everywhere but on my face. She raised her hands to my shirt and started undoing the buttons.

As many times as I'd imagined this moment, I'd never pictured a room full of people and the tang of apple filling the air. When she started to pull my shirttails out of my pants, I brushed her hands away. "Stop. I don't need help." Mabel's cheeks colored. *Interesting, probably due to the warmth of the room.* "I'll wash the shirt in whatever trough I find."

Chapter 7

Once Upon a Time in the Plot
Love's Gamble

"Of course. I'm sorry." My gaze followed the tattoo on Sam's shoulder as he stalked across the room. Why did it fascinate me so? I suppose because it was so at odds with the Sam I'd grown comfortable with. He slipped out a side door and I released the breath I'd been holding.

I didn't feel like dancing anymore, though Mom and Dad were still kicking up their heels. I needed to see if I could make some headway with Beau. The sooner he self-realized, the sooner Sam and I could get back to the real world.

I felt a little guilty making him tag along for my adventure, but I liked that I could talk about all the weird stuff with him. As my oldest friend, I enjoyed Sam's company and trusted him to steer me in the right direction, even though I had a history of not taking his advice.

Beau rejoined me. "I thank you for the dance, Rose. I trust the ranger here will see you safely home." He nodded over my shoulder.

I turned, but no one stood behind me.

Beau continued talking. "Much obliged." He stuck out his hand and mimed a handshake. "You keep me informed if Cutter shows his face around Rosie's ranch again." He nodded. "I will."

It was incredibly weird to watch someone carry on a conversation with air.

He looked at me and tipped his hat. "Miss Rose. I'll call on you later this week."

"Uhh, thanks?"

Beau walked off and left me standing alone, well, other than all the other cowboys and ladies milling around me. So much for drawing him into a conversation. This was going to be more difficult than my mother made it sound.

I located my parents on the dance floor and said my goodbyes, then hurried to catch up with Sam.

He stood at a wooden trough surrounded by horses. His back muscles flexed as he wrung water out of his shirt. Again, the tattoo drew my attention. I shook my head to clear the errant thoughts.

"Sam, are you ready to go?"

"More than. I don't know if I'll be colder shirtless or wearing this wet." He frowned.

I unwrapped the shawl that came with my character. "Here. Just wear this."

Sam hesitated.

"Don't worry. None of the other cowboys will tease you. I doubt this is part of the script."

With resignation, he lifted the gray wool from my fingers and wound it around his neck like a scarf. I didn't comment. Once he got over being embarrassed and started feeling the night chill, he'd wear it properly. Until then I'd have to ignore my good friend's exposed chest and abs.

"I'll walk you to the wagon. Where'd you park?"

I pointed across the yard.

"I don't suppose you made it to the store." He guided me by my elbow around horses and wagons. We paused as an older couple crossed our path, followed by two young women.

"Good night, Ranger," they chorused and gave shy waves. "I hope we'll see you around town," the taller girl added.

"I hope we'll see you around town," I mimicked in a high-pitched voice and rolled my eyes.

Sam tipped his hat. "Have a good night, ladies." He smirked at me. "If I didn't know better, I'd accuse you of being jealous."

"Hardly," I scoffed. "They're just such obviously scripted characters, I find them silly." I really wanted to scoff again to emphasize my point, but that might've been overkill.

"Right. Why would you be jealous?" Sam mumbled.

It occurred to me Sam might be experiencing jealousy himself. I've met the man of my dreams and soon would ride off into the sunset with my hero sheriff. Poor Sam didn't date much and was hopelessly awkward outside of the swimming pool. I wondered how often he even left the library. Maybe he was afraid our relationship would change when I married real-life Beau and moved on without him.

I touched Sam's arm. "Sam." He paused his steps. "Even after I get married, we'll still be best friends. I'll help you get set up on some dating sites and be your dating coach."

I couldn't read all the expressions that crossed his face, but the last looked like resignation. "I appreciate it, Mabes, but I don't need any dating help. I'll know the right girl if I meet her." He resumed walking. "So, did you get the supplies?"

"No. The horse brought me straight here. Ugh. That means we're going to have to come back tomorrow." Fatigue settled on my shoulders and my feet dragged as we approached the wagon.

"Maybe not. Thank *you*, magic." A smile spread across Sam's face.

I peeked over the side of our wagon. The bottom was filled with wooden crates and cloth sacks, presumably full of…ingredients. Biting back an ungracious remark, I said weakly, "Yeah. Let's hope Rose's mom has a cookbook back at the house." An unexpected yawn escaped.

Sam nudged my shoulder. "Come on. I'll drive. Can't have you passing out and toppling off your seat."

****

"Mabel, wake up. We're home."

I bolted upright at Sam's words. The endless expanse of velvety darkness and twinkling stars killed my dream of being snuggled on the sofa in my apartment.

"Go in and get ready for bed. I'll unload the groceries." He began unhitching the team from the wagon.

"I can help. I'll start carrying everything in while you take care of the horses." My little dog came running from somewhere and danced around Sam's feet. The poor guy needed a name. "Will you feed Scamp, too?"

"Scamp?" I could barely make out Sam's questioning look in the moonlight.

I shrugged. "I feel like I should call him something. I don't know if he actually needs to eat but see if there's anything with the horse food."

I stood on shaky legs and Sam hurried to help me down out of the wagon. My shawl settled more appropriately over his shoulders. I placed my hands on them as he lifted me down, remembering how they'd looked earlier.

"Scamp is as good a name as any, I suppose." He set me on the ground, close enough to feel the heat emanating from his torso. He unwound the shawl and handed it to me. "Here. This is pretty impractical for barn chores. Thank you. When the breeze kicked up, I was glad to have it."

Overtired and overcome, tears pinched my eyes. I wrapped my arms around Sam and pressed my cheek to his chest. "I don't know how I'd manage if you weren't here with me. You're the best person I know. I love you so much."

His arms wrapped around me, and he tucked my head under his chin into the curve of his neck. I felt his Adam's apple bob as he swallowed before speaking. "I love you, too. I'll always be here for you, no matter what." After a second, he released me and pulled away. "Don't try to carry in any of the crates or big sacks. Between the darkness and your long dress, you're liable to get tripped up."

I immediately missed his warmth, but the sooner we finished the chores, the sooner we could put this interminable day behind us.

Sam joined me shortly, explaining that when he went to untack the second horse, he found it and his own mount already brushed down and munching on fresh hay. Scamp, likewise, rested on a pile of rags with a bone. Unfortunately, our luck did not stretch to magically unloading all the groceries and figuring out where to store them. We left most of it on the table and sideboards, hoping the plot didn't include mice or other vermin.

"I thought Rose lived here with her parents. Why is there only one bed?" Sam, now wearing a Henley-style pullover, stared into the bedroom with his hands planted on his hips.

"I don't know. I skimmed a lot of the boring backstory." I shrugged. "We can share, or you can take the floor."

"I'm the one here against my will. I'm not sleeping on the floor. That bed is barely more than a twin. How did Rose's parents even sleep there?"

I shrugged again, too tired to care. "It's not like we've never slept together before."

"We're not little kids anymore, Mabes." His eyes met mine and heat crept up my neck.

"Just get in bed, Sam. Quit making such a big deal about it." I found the button to my skirt and began the process of disrobing. "I'll be sure to email the author about the huge one-bed plot hole when we get back."

"What are you doing? You can't take your clothes off," Sam sputtered.

With a stomp of my foot and a twist of my hips, the skirt pooled at my feet. "Watch me." My fingers moved to my blouse.

"Mabel." Sam's warning tone had zero effect on me.

"Sam," I mocked. "I am wearing at least four layers of clothing. I am only taking off three. Quit being such a prude. You've spent half your time here at least half naked, so hush." I whipped off my blouse and tossed it in the corner. A sleeveless slip and some sort of bloomers were all that remained. Four layers may have been an exaggeration. I opted to take off the bloomers and use the slip as a nightgown. Miss Rose would be commando as well, but so be it. I'd be asleep before my head hit the pillow.

Chapter 8

Rude Awakening
Love's Gamble

A wild hog grunting in my ear startled me out of my nightmare, where I was losing a battle with a giant squid. The wild appendages followed me from the dreamworld as I thrashed to free myself from the beast. Landing at last on the floor, I peered over the edge of the bed, expecting to see the hog wallowing in my spot.

Mabel lay there like a starfish. I jumped again when she emitted a grunting snore loud enough to shake the rafters. I grinned. It was a new quirk since the last time we'd shared sleeping quarters. I didn't need to worry about a wild hog, only a bed hog. The desire to climb in and join her made me move from the floor. The realization that I was, once again, shirtless, directed my steps to the bureau instead of back to bed.

Lamenting the missed opportunity, I shook Mabel's exposed foot. "Mabel, time to get up."

She groaned and curled into a ball like a kitten. "Nooo, Sam."

At least she had an awareness of who she was with. "Mabes. The sooner we start our day and find out what the plot has in store, the sooner we can go home."

She threw the sheet aside. "Ugh. I can't believe we're still here."

I pulled a clean shirt out of the drawer, buttoned it, and tucked it into the jeans I'd worn to bed. Feeling a jab in my pants pocket, I pulled out my ranger badge and pinned it to the new shirt. Weird how it found its way back to my pocket.

"Get dressed. I'm going to see if I can figure out how to make breakfast." The pie and cider from the previous evening had provided temporary fulfillment at best.

"Mmm. Frosted strawberry toaster pastries, please," Mabel mumbled.

"I'll see what I can do." She sat up, exorcist-style, in bed. I left before her head could start spinning.

Stifling a yawn, I headed to the kitchen area. While Mabel fell asleep quickly the night before, I tossed and turned, constantly aware of her body next to mine. How many times had I dreamed of just that situation? When would I come to terms with the fact that Mabel would never be for me? I'd think she and Sheriff Beau two-stepping all over my heart would do the trick.

Thankfully, the kitchen had been magicked to rights overnight. A basket of eggs sat on the wooden sideboard next to a huge slab of meat. Two thin cuts lay beside it. Bacon. Since I had not recognized the meat as such, I appreciated the magic tutorial.

By the time Mabel staggered into the room, a plate of half-blackened bacon and greasy fried eggs awaited her. She eyed my offering skeptically as she slumped into a chair.

"If you put it between two slices of bread, it's not bad. You can cook tomorrow."

"I'm hoping to not be here tomorrow." She forked eggs and bacon onto bread.

"How does the saying go? Hope for the best…"

Penny Ante: The Good, the Bad, and the Romance

With a resigned sigh she finished, "Plan for the worst. I wonder what happens today? I hope my mom appreciated how handy it was to have your mom read ahead for her. I feel like we're flying blind."

I sat down across from Mabel. "It makes me uncomfortable, too. I keep reminding myself what you said about the magic not hurting us and working for the good of the women in your family. I really hope that includes best friends of women in your family."

"Your mom and dad never had any trouble that I recall." She paused. "Just sore muscles, I think."

The house rattled when someone pounded on the door.

I rose. "Stay here."

Mabel pushed back from the table and followed. "It's my house."

In a few giant steps, I beat her to the door and pulled it open, blocking her from the entrance. "Can I help you gentlemen?"

Three men of varying ages and degrees of cleanliness stood on the porch. My horse, saddled and ready to go, was tied to the railing. The oldest man spoke. "Miss Rose, I hate to bring ya bad news so early in the morning, but we was out riding the fence line and it 'peers it's been cut."

The shortest man stepped forward. "It looks like it 'twere vandals. No lying."

I shifted so Rose could squeeze in beside me, which she did with a glare in my direction.

"Oh, no! Who do you think did it?" she asked.

The older man's gaze shifted to me. "Cain't tell till we do a count. Maybe ten or fifteen. Jeb and Slim are out there now, makin' sure no more escape." He looked back at Mabel. "I wanted to tell ya that's where we'll all be today. Fixin' the hole, checkin' for more, and countin' the head."

The short man smiled and nodded at me. "Much 'bliged, Ranger. We sure could use the extra hands."

I turned to Mabel. "I guess I know what I'm doing today."

****

Sweat ran down my brow as I lifted my canteen to my lips. We'd only been working a couple hours, yet what was left of my shirt was drenched in perspiration. The men's conclusion of vandalism, even to my untrained eye, appeared correct. The barbed wire fencing had been cut clean through in several places, so it couldn't be repaired. It had to be replaced.

Between collecting all the cuttings and dealing with the springy spool of new wire, my shirt had been ripped to shreds. I refused to remove it on principle.

"Thar's Miss Rose." One of the hands pointed toward a rider coming across the field from the direction of the house.

Had something happened at the house? Earlier, after some debate, Mabel conceded to stay at the ranch house since my horse was the only one magically saddled. I didn't like leaving her alone with Jace, the antagonist, still unaccounted for. I'd given her a quick recap of my visit with the sheriff the night before and told her to keep the shotgun by the door.

Now, she carried the shotgun and a picnic basket on her lap. She smiled, reached a hand up to wave, then quickly returned it to the basket when it started to slip. I'd missed her in the few hours we'd been apart, and a return smile rose to my lips.

I walked to meet her a few yards from the group of ranch hands. "Everything okay?" I relieved her of the basket and gun.

"Yep. I followed Scamp around the homestead for a while. I figured I should be familiar with what all the buildings were. We found the chicken coop and I collected more eggs. When I got back to the house, the picnic basket sat on the table and ham, cheese, and bread lay on the counter. When my stomach growled, I figured the magic hinted I should bring you, and them, lunch." She nodded at the hands affixing the last length of wire to a post. "Do they even eat?"

"They've been drinking water right along with me, so probably."

"That basket is stuffed full of sandwiches. I didn't know what else to bring. It's not like there were any potato chips with the stuff we brought in last night. What happened to your shirt?"

"The magic seems determined to relieve me of it."

Mabel snorted. "I don't think that's how it works."

I set the basket down on a stump, grabbing a sandwich off the top before the other hands converged on it. I gave Mabel a side eye. "But you don't really know how it works anymore, do you?"

"Touché." She shaded her eyes and looked across the field. A rider on a white horse approached at a fast clip. The sun glinted off the badge on the rider's shirt, confirming his identity.

"Of course, he rides a white horse," I grumbled.

Mabel brushed the wrinkles out of her skirt and smoothed her hair. "How do I look?"

Gorgeous, fresh, happy. "Fine."

"Pfft. You're no help." She fluffed the hair she just

smoothed. I couldn't tell the difference. "I have to get him to break character."

"I'll try to help, but it didn't go so well for me last night."

"Maybe I'm the one who has to get him to do it." She pinched her cheeks as Sheriff Beau rode up.

He swung his body gracefully out of the saddle and landed next to Mabel. "Rose, I'm glad to find you unharmed. I worried when you weren't at the house."

Mabel literally batted her eyelashes at the man. "What's wrong, sheriff? We had a spot of trouble this morning. My men discovered damage to the fence and missing cattle. I've just brought them sandwiches. Would you care for one?"

"Your neighbor, Pat Burton, caught me near the church. He reported seeing a few head he recognized as yours out by the pond on his property. He would'a got 'em for you, but he was bringin' his mother to church. You know how Ma Burton can't abide being late for preachin'."

Mabel nodded, her lips pursed in annoyance. She put a hand on his arm. "Yes, yes, but would you like a sandwich?"

One of the ranch hands spoke. "Yes, Miss Rose. I'll run get those varmints right now." He headed toward his horse.

Beau turned to me. "Do you think this is Cutter's work? Things have been quiet in town. Too many people are being paid to keep quiet," he added ominously.

This guy was a tough nut. "I believe the lady offered you a sandwich. Twice."

Beau nodded. "I agree. If he undermines her operation and she loses money, she'll have no choice but to sell, and possibly at below value."

I glanced at Mabel, whose pursed lips now frowned. But Beau wasn't done.

"I'd feel more comfortable if Rose would move to town. Widow Spencer has offered to put her up."

Mabel stomped her foot. "It's not up to either of you where I stay. I am not cattle!"

I grinned. "You mean chattel?"

"What's chattel?"

"It's property."

"I'm not that either. Apparently, Beau's not ready to self-realize. I'm going back to the house." She flounced to her horse and climbed on smoothly as the horsewoman she was.

The sheriff's gaze followed Mabel's tirade and dramatic exit. Maybe he wasn't as far from self-realizing as Mabel thought.

Chapter 9

What the Blazes?
Love's Gamble

The nerve! It felt good to ride out my frustration. By the time I reached the house, I'd almost forgiven Beau for being such a misogynistic jerk. So maybe my feelings were a little hurt that he still didn't recognize me as his true love.

It took my dad all the way till the end of the book to come out of his character's stupor. I assumed it would be easier for me since I had the benefit of foreknowledge about the true situation. It's true what they say about what happens when you assume.

I rode straight into the barn, ready to tackle the comforting task of caring for my horse. "I suppose I should give you a name, too." I pulled off the bridle. "You have brown eyes like Bertie, and I really wish I could talk to her right now." The saddle weighed a ton. I wasn't sure where it went, so I balanced it on the side of the stall. "Besides, she'll never know I named you after her."

Horse Bertie nibbled my hair as I ran the curry comb down her neck and back. "The man of my dreams, well, to be honest, I never dreamed of anyone quite like Beau. I should probably call him my soul mate. He doesn't feel like a soul mate yet, though. Anyway, I'm super-attracted to him, but I don't feel a connection yet. I wish I'd asked Mom more questions."

Scamp wandered into the barn, snuffling the ground. I continued my counseling session with Bertie. "And Sam is acting very un-Sam-like. I feel really bad that he got pulled along for the ride, but I'm glad he's here. Though he's not being very helpful with Beau. He acts like he doesn't like him, which, I suppose, is how Sam normally feels about my boyfriends. He seems sad this time, though."

Scamp finished his sniffing, gave a growl and a yip, and ran out of the barn.

"And what the heck is up with me? Sam is like a brother and all of a sudden, I'm noticing him. I'm trying not to let it distract me. It would probably help if Beau would take his shirt off, too.

"I need to be a better friend to Sam and, at the same time, stop ogling his chest. Easier said than—hey!" Bertie sidestepped, nearly tromping on my feet. She nickered and stepped into me again. "Shh. What's the matter, girl?" A faint whisp of smoke reached my nose.

While I'd been intent on my heart to heart with my horse, the front of the barn filled with smoke. Small piles of hay had spilled or been dragged across the entrance. How had I not heard that happening? Stupid plot! Flames jumped from pile to pile, and sparks floated up to more flammable junk in the loft overhead. Bertie and I weren't getting out that way.

I could hear Scamp outside, barking his little head off. Poor guy tried to warn me earlier. Was I off-plot now? Should I have followed the dog to safety when I still had the chance? *The magic won't let me die. The magic won't let me die.*

My mind sped through dozens of options with a conspiracy theory thrown in for good measure. First, get myself and the two horses out. I hoped there weren't any other livestock in the barn besides my wagon horses.

Second, worry about how the fire started. Nothing I'd done could have contributed to it. There were no lit lamps or woodstoves nearby. That meant arson. And that meant Jace, our antagonist, was close.

So, third, be ready to protect myself when I got out of the barn. And maybe see about trying to put the fire out.

These thoughts sped through my mind as I returned to Bertie. "I've always wanted to do this." I reached down and tore a large section from the bottom of my dress. The rending noise added to Bertie's panic. "It's okay, girl. We're getting out right now." I dipped the fabric in a pail of water and tied it around my nose and mouth. Two stalls down, the other horse kicked at its walls.

Bertie followed me without having to be tied. Thank goodness for small favors. "Come on." I led her to the back double doors of the barn. "I'll be back for you, horse," I told the other mount. I trusted Bertie to follow, but I wouldn't put it past the other panicked mare to trample me.

I reached the back doors and shoved. Of course, nothing happened. I didn't unfasten the latch. It took two hands to lift the old, warped wood out of the way. If I didn't burn to death, I'd have several splinters to deal with later.

Shoving the door again, this time it swayed outward, but the equally warped bottom refused to budge. I could squeeze out and save myself. The fresh air blowing in made me realize how thick the smoke had become inside. Bertie pawed at the ground. Fictional or not, I couldn't leave the animals behind.

This time, I shoved and kicked the bottom at the same time. The door flew open, and Bertie bumped me as she galloped to safety. The other horse screamed behind me. Adjusting my mask, I headed back into the thickening smoke to rescue her.

****

Sheriff Beau left not long after Mabel. I couldn't decide if his reaction was to her or to Rose behaving similarly in the storyline. Like Mabel, strong heroines also didn't appreciate being protected like fragile dolls.

I reached for another sandwich and noticed Mabel's shotgun still leaning on the stump. Its presence reeked of foreshadowing. I grabbed the gun and ran for my horse.

Scamp met me on the trail in the middle of a copse of scrub oaks. "What's the matter, Lassie? Is Mabel stuck in the well?" I joked with the mutt but quickened my horse's pace. The scent of smoke reached me moments before I broke from the trees. I didn't need a narrator to tell me the odds of Mabel being in the burning barn.

Smoke billowing from both ends suggested both sets of doors were open. My gut told me Mabel was still in trouble. She might be stuck inside or injured. I angled my horse to the rear of the barn, hoping the flames were confined to the front. I barely registered the two wagon horses grazing on the lawn as I rode by.

At the back of the barn I dismounted, pulling a bandana from my pocket as I went. I dragged it through a water trough and tied it around my face. "Mabel!" *I am an English scholar. I am a swimmer; fire is my nemesis.*

I have never been anyone's hero. I shoved away the negative thoughts before they could spiral me into inaction. "Mabel!" I ran into the burning building…and tripped over a body.

"Sam!" Cough, cough. "You idiot," Mabel rasped. "Get down."

Since falling over her put me 'down,' I crawled closer to her. "Are you hurt? I'm trying to rescue you." Cough, cough.

She pointed to where the light spilled in from the doors. "Out." Cough.

I nodded and followed her snail-like pace, resisting the urge to pick her up and run. After the third time her long skirts caused her to faceplant, I did just that. We were within twenty feet of the exit, and I had enough adrenaline to make it happen. The fire was getting too hot on my backside for me to feel comfortable crawling any longer.

We collapsed outside in the grass. I pulled off her mask and smoothed back her hair, then checked her for burns and broken bones.

She feebly smacked my hands away between hacking coughs. "I'm fine. Horse knocked me down. Stunned for a minute. Crawling out."

Removing my mask, I breathed a clean sigh of relief. "This is not how it's supposed to go." I yelled at the sky. "Do you hear me, magic? Stop effing with our lives and send us home!"

Mabel put her hand on my arm. Cough. "Sam. It's okay." Cough. "My fault."

"You started the fire?"

She shook her head. "Know better. Panicked horses."

I pulled her onto my lap and wrapped my arms around her. We were both sooty messes. "None of this is your fault. You didn't ask to be here and the magic needs to quit playing fast and loose with your life." Deep below the smoke, I could still pick up a hint of her shampoo.

She relaxed against me, and my heart rate finally settled. Now that my pulse stopped pounding in my ears, I picked up the sounds of people at the front of the barn. "Can you walk?"

Cough. "Don't you dare carry me."

Rising, I pulled Mabel to her feet. "Do you think it's the fire department?"

At the front of the barn, a line of people, presumably neighbors, spread out from the well to form a bucket brigade. Actually, more of a saucepan, kettle, chamber pot, bucket brigade.

Assuring myself the chamber pot was surely unused, I joined the line to save Mabel's, er, Rose's barn. Mabel joined the line conveying empty containers back to the well. I kept one eye on her and one on my task until a man closer to the barn declared the fire defeated.

Cheers went up around us and we shook hands and thanked our neighbors for their help with promises to have families over to share a meal soon. I received a few askance glances from the women and realized my tattered shirt left little to pin my ranger badge to and even less to the imagination.

I turned to shake another hand and met a familiar face.

"I'm just glad Miss Rose had her *cousin* here to save her. Terrible, terrible things can befall a woman living alone this far from town." Jace Cutter tipped his hat and sauntered to his horse.

Before I could wrap my brain around the ramifications of Cutter's presence, my quarry was gone.

Chapter 10

Lonely is the Hero
Love's Gamble

The adrenaline rush had long since worn off by the time the neighbors left, and Mabel and I could retreat to the house. I checked the barn and found the animals all put up and happily munching their dinners. My stomach growled, and I groaned at the reminder our own dinner would not be as simple as heating up a pizza.

When I stepped inside, Mabel stood at the stove ladling beef and root vegetables out of a cast iron Dutch oven. "You cooked?"

She laughed. "Not hardly. Despite its attempt to kill me off today, the magic made sure we didn't starve to death. This was bubbling on the stovetop when I came in. Here." She handed me a heaping bowl.

I looked down at myself, then at her. "You don't think we should clean up first?"

A blush rose on her cheeks. "I don't have the energy to deal with the tub right now. After dinner will be soon enough."

I took the bowl and thanked her. She joined me at the table, placing a mug of milk in front of me. I picked out a small piece of straw floating on top. "We have cows?"

Mabel shrugged. "There was a bucket of milk on the counter. Be warned, it isn't skim or low fat." She took a sip from her own mug, then licked away a milk mustache. "Fictional calories don't count." Her smile lightened the heaviness I'd been carrying from the exhausting day.

The pot roast smelled amazing, and the taste reminded me of meals our families had shared on camping trips. Everything tasted better when cooked outdoors, and Dutch oven was one of my favorite outdoor cooking methods.

I ate in silence until I could no longer feel hunger clawing at my insides. "Jace Cutter was in the crowd this afternoon. Did you see him?"

She dabbed at her mouth with a cloth napkin. "No, but I'm not surprised. My list of enemies is short, as in one. That fire couldn't have started without help. Why didn't you nab him?"

"He took me by surprise. He made a veiled threat about your safety, but I think I have to catch him in the act of doing something nefarious."

"I thought there was a wanted poster."

I pushed away from the table in irritation. "If I was supposed to catch him, as you say, then he would have held out his hands for me to cuff him, or whatever. He said his lines and left, so it was not time for him to be apprehended. Besides, if your sheriff is the hero in all this, he's probably going to be the one to do it. Not me."

I stalked out the back door and picked up the washtub from its spot by the house. I carried it in and set it next to the wood stove, hoping it would magically fill again.

"Sam…"

I didn't want her pity or her apology. "You go first. I'm going to go check on the animals and around the property. Yell at me when you're through." I slammed the door behind me before she could respond.

Mabel found me later, sitting on the front porch with Scamp. I'd thought about trying to whittle but settled for identifying constellations in the fictional sky. Her hair hung in damp ringlets around her face, and she wore a light blue cotton and lace nightie that covered her neck to toes. Probably for the best. The outfit screamed 'don't touch' and would remind my fingers not to reach for her enticing curls.

"I'm done. The water is still hot. Putting it by the stove was a good idea. I set some clothes out for you. If you wash those pants tonight and hang them by the fire, they'll probably be dry by morning." She hesitated on the threshold, hand still on the doorknob.

"Thanks. I'll be right in."

"Do you want me to try to shave you?"

I couldn't see her in the darkness, backlit as she was. Unable to discern her true feeling about the idea, I scratched at the thickening scruff on my face. It drove me nuts; I don't remember the last time I let it get so long. But picturing that folding blade made me shudder. "No. I'm fine."

"Okay. It makes you look older. I mean, not old, just…uh, different. I like it. The other way is good, too."

"Mabes?" Why was she rambling about my beard?

"I'll just be in bed. Goodnight." She stepped back into the house and shut the door.

****

I slipped into the steaming tub, groaning as each ache and pain slipped below the surface. The only indication of Mabel's having bathed was the lingering scent of roses. Cuts from the barbed wire and scrapes from the barn burned anew as I ran the bar of soap over my skin. I treated my hair, face, and beard likewise, thankful the magic provided me a masculine smelling bar rather than the floral one Mabel used.

Lamenting the lack of clean water, I rinsed as best I could and toweled dry. Tucking the cloth around my waist, I emptied my pants pockets, finding a knife, hanky, and my ranger badge. I dunked the denim in the wash tub, agitating and rubbing away any visible dirt. After ringing them dry, I draped them over a chair near the stove.

I glanced at the bedroom door, then donned the long john bottoms Mabel left for me. I carried the shirt with me back to the bedroom. With a light knock, I asked, "Mabel? Can I come in?"

"Of course," came the muffled reply.

I pushed open the door. Mabel lay in bed with the covers pulled up to her chin. "Are you all right?" I moved to the dresser.

"I'm fine. Super tired. Why aren't you wearing a shirt?"

"With the rate I've been going through them, I thought it best to preserve when possible. I don't normally wear anything to bed." Mabel made a small choking sound. "So, I'm going to put this back and hope it doesn't disappear by morning." I turned to her. "Are you sure you're okay?"

"I'm fine, Sam. Just get in bed." She rolled on her side, giving me her back.

I doused the lamp and climbed into bed, hoping to get some solid sleep in before Mabel woke me with her flailing and snores.

****

I had been on the edge of sleep when Sam knocked on the door. Darn that man and his naked chest! It made me think of Sam as a man and not my friend. Every time I saw those chiseled swimmers' muscles, it became more difficult to shove him back in the friend box. Beau needed to hurry up and claim me.

And what in the world possessed me to offer to shave him? My mouth seems to have slipped its leash along with my wayward thoughts. Though, removing the beard would make him look more like my Sam again. At this point, I didn't know how much that would help.

I lay there exhausted, but awake, listening to Sam's breathing slow. He worked much harder than I did today; much harder than he was used to as well. Thank goodness he was fit. Sooo fit. I expelled a breath and rolled to my other side. Moonlight through the window softly lit his features, damp hair combed back from his face, and dark lashes resting on his cheeks.

An inhalation filled my nose with the scent of woodsy soap and Sam's own comforting smell. I wouldn't take advantage of his friendship while we were in the story, though the plot seemed to have no such qualms. I wouldn't make him help me with Beau anymore, though. With magic going haywire, I didn't know if real world time continued to move or stopped while we were in-book, like my parents' experience. It wasn't fair to make Sam put his life on hold. I'd use everything in my power to get Beau's attention next time I saw him so we could move on.

Satisfied with my plan, I closed my eyes, determined to make sleep come. Finally, I laid my hand on Sam's arm to anchor my tumultuous thoughts and drifted to sleep.

Chapter 11

Red Herring's Errand
Love's Gamble

I awoke in a sweat. I had no idea what month it was in book-world, but my understanding held that in Texas it was hot most of the time anyway. It was too warm for the voluminous nightie hitched up around one thigh and wrapped boa constrictor-style around the other. And way too warm for the heat emanating from the chest I mistook for a pillow.

Sam's even breathing told me he still slept. Thank goodness. I just needed to get away without waking him. When I lifted my head, the arm I hadn't noticed around my waist tightened. I held my breath. I tried again, easing my body out from under his arm and wriggling to the end of the bed.

Escape accomplished, I checked on my captor. Sam rolled over into the spot I'd occupied and emitted a soft snore. With cautious looks over my shoulder, I quickly whipped off the offending gown and donned clean undergarments and a dress. Sam remained asleep. The least I could do was manage breakfast for us this morning.

Ingredients were piled on the countertop and a stained recipe card lay in the middle of the table. Biscuits and gravy. Thank you, magic.

Assessing what I had to work with, I thanked the

magic again. If forced to identify lard on my own, amongst a pantry full of foodstuffs, I would have come up lacking. Flour and labeled tins were easy in comparison. I'd made biscuits with vegetable shortening before but didn't care to delve too deeply into lard's origins.

As I formed the dough, my mind wandered to what the plot had in store for us today. I hoped Beau would come around and that Sam would have something entertaining to do. Based on the book's title, *Love's Gamble*, I assumed there would be some card playing in my future. Maybe Beau would be forced to save my life by winning a card game. I don't know what series of events could lead to that happening, but anything was possible.

Sam emerged from the bedroom, wearing a shirt, and stretching as I pulled the slightly overdone biscuits from the oven. "Smells good. Better than burnt bacon."

"Sorry, no meat this morning. You'll get your protein from the eggs." I dumped the scrambled eggs into the thickening gravy and removed the skillet from the stove.

Sam stood next to me. His stomach growled. "I'm not complaining. You did a better job than I did."

"The magic probably thought I needed more help than you. Sit down, and I'll fix you a plate."

Sam pulled out a chair and sat at the table. "We should probably eat fast just in case we get visitors again this morning."

I set a plate in front of him and another at my spot. "Bite your tongue. I don't know the exact formula for romances, but it seems like after two hits on my land by Jace, something should escalate. Otherwise, the story would be stagnant. Right? You study this stuff."

He shifted in his seat. "Well, not this exactly, but I've taken a class on the genre."

"Then what do you think happens next, professor?" I took a bite of my breakfast. Not bad, I totally nailed it.

Sam's face, the parts not covered by beard, and neck turned red. "I don't really know the heat level of this book. If it's a sweet romance, then yes, we're probably close to moving on to escalation by the villain."

"I don't generally read sweet, to be honest. What does that change?"

He cleared his throat and took another bite, chewing it thoroughly before answering. "For anything above sweet, there are usually some romantic clinches, or, um, sex, before the antagonist does their thing. So, you can probably expect a visit and maybe a, uh, kiss or something from the sheriff today." Sam stared intently at his plate while shoveling in another mouthful.

"Oh." Clever response, that. I should feel really excited about the prospect of kissing Beau. It was weird because I didn't know him at all. I'd be kissing the character. On the other hand, maybe it was just the opportunity I needed to spark his self-realization. "What are you doing today?"

"Unless the magic directs me otherwise, I guess I'll go check the fence we repaired yesterday and help the ranch hands with their duties."

A scratching came at the door, followed by a yip. Scamp! I swear he was the easiest dog to own. I didn't have to feed him, scoop his messes, or evidently, remember his existence.

"I'll get it." Sam wiped his face and scraped his chair back from the table.

He opened the door and Scamp pranced in to greet me. I gave him a pat, and he settled at my feet. I must not be in grave danger at the moment.

Sam still stood at the door. "My horse is out here, saddled. Guess I'll finish getting dressed." He shut the door, grabbed his jeans from the chair by the stove, and disappeared into the bedroom.

I stood and began to clear the table. Scamp remained underneath the table and curled up to take a nap. "Looks like Sam gets all the excitement today."

About thirty minutes after Sam left, Scamp perked up and ran to the door. I'd finished cleaning up and prepared myself for a boring morning. The gun leaned on the wall near the door, but Scamp didn't act aggressively toward whatever was happening outside. I shrugged and walked to the door and my fate.

I pulled open the door just as a lady knocked the air where it had been. There were two of them, both in calico bonnets and dresses. They ignored me for a moment, giggling with each other, then looked up as if I had answered the door…which I had…several beats ago. Characters were so annoying.

"Good morning, Rose. Is the ranger in?" One of the girls simpered. Yes, simpered. I could not have described a simper before that moment, but the girl definitely did it.

"Nope. He's out." No need to elaborate since Sam didn't even know what his plans were.

She continued, "Oh, that's too bad. Beth and I brought him some fresh baked shortbread to help him regain his strength after his trying day yesterday."

"Perfect! I had an exceptionally trying day yesterday, too." Yum, shortbread!

"Do you know when he'll return?" Beth asked, making no move to hand over the treat.

"No idea. Hand over the baked goods and no one will get hurt."

The girls nodded sympathetically to whatever Rose said, then adopted furtive expressions. Uh oh.

"We heard Sheriff Wilson plans to offer for you as soon as you're out of mourning," not-Beth said.

"He's such a good man to wait for so long," Beth added.

I supposed these girls, women, whatever were about Rose's age and were probably friends in the story.

"Really? Why wouldn't you? Why every single woman in town would snap up a catch like the sheriff," Beth said.

"A few of the married ones, too." Not-Beth giggled.

Where was this going? If Beau was the hero, why was Rose having second thoughts?

Beth spoke again, "Not us, of course. Not as long as Ranger McGrath is around."

Through gritted teeth I said, "I'll be sure to let the ranger know you came by." I snatched the shortbread from Beth's hands—I'm not ashamed—and shut the door in their faces.

****

I rode for twenty minutes in a direction neither toward town nor the pastures where I'd worked yesterday. It gave me time to delve into all my stored writing knowledge and apply it to my conversation with Mabel, primarily my role in the story.

Things happened to Mabel when she was alone. Her interactions at the dance hall and the fire were good examples. Whenever anything of consequence happened to me, I was with Mabel...or Beau. So, if the story is being told from dual points of view, Rose's and Beau's, where does that leave me? Not to mention, Beau seemed to already have a relationship with Rose. I could just be there to give Beau incentive to make his move.

What was the point of my current field trip? If something happened at the house with Mabel, this only served to get me out of the scene. But, if I was riding *to* something, an event or encounter with Jace, then that will prove I'm the second point of view in the story.

My heart leapt in realization. If I'm the second POV, that makes me Rose's hero and love interest. Why would the magic go through the trouble? If Mabel was going to see me as something other than a friend, it would have happened before now.

Still, I couldn't quite squelch the hope in my chest as I rode on, watching for a destination to clarify my character's existence.

Ten minutes later, my hopes were dashed when I arrived at a small bluff overlooking a run-down cabin. A familiar white horse stood hobbled a short distance away. I left my horse with the sheriff's mount, not bothering to tether it. If the plot wanted it to run away, it would, regardless.

"Looks like your hunch was correct. There are two to three men holed up in that cabin, but I haven't been able to identify Cutter yet," Beau said as I approached.

I knelt beside him behind a conveniently placed log and peered at the cabin. A lean-to stuck out the back of the cabin and may have housed horses. A shadow moved in front of one of the windows, and Beau tensed.

Beau unstrapped one of the two belts he wore and handed it to me. "I didn't figure your weapon ever turned up. This belonged to my last deputy, may he rest in peace. You can use it as long as you're here, but it belongs to the town, now."

I strapped the gun belt around my waist and examined the piece. It was a similar revolver to one Uncle Tripp had trained us on. I checked the cylinder and found it loaded.

The sheriff motioned for me to follow him as he crept from our hiding spot and made our way down to some scraggly bushes, then to a broken-down wagon. "You surprise them at the front door after I get into position in the back. When we split off, give me until a count of sixty to get ready."

We continued toward the house in plain view of anyone happening to look out the window. Beau gave me a shove in the direction of the front door as his hunched figure hurried to the back. I, too, was hunched in an effort to keep a low profile until I remembered it didn't make a lick of difference and straightened. I'd forgotten to count but decided that didn't much matter either.

As I reached for the doorknob, I heard commotion within, and feet pounding toward the back. I'd missed my cue. Oh well. I opened the door and ran through the house and out the back in time to see Beau tying the hands of one man and another unconscious on the ground. Neither were Jace Cutter.

"Did Jace get away?" I asked.

Beau looked at me. "Good question. Where *is* Jace Cutter?"

Chapter 12

A Woman Who Plays Games
Love's Gamble

After the girls left, I paced the floor, munching shortbread and waiting on Sam. When he strode out of the bedroom that morning in his stiff jeans and shiny badge pinned to a blue plaid shirt, I told myself he'd be fine. The magic wouldn't hurt him. It didn't keep me from worrying, though.

I heard a horse come to a stop out front. I hastily wrapped my ill-gotten treat and brushed crumbs from my face and dress. Boot steps sounded on the porch, then a knock at the door. Sam wouldn't knock. It had to be Beau.

I pasted a smile on my face and threw open the door.

"Darlin', a man could get used to that kind of welcome," Jace Cutter drawled.

My smile fled. "What do you want?"

Cutter smirked. "I like a woman who don't play games. I want the same as I always want; more. You don't need this farm. Your parents didn't think you'd have any other choices, bluestocking that you are."

I tapped my foot in irritation. "Rude. What are you going to do about it?"

He stood in silence for a moment, contemplating whatever scripted lines Rose fed him.

"That doesn't seem fair to you. I wouldn't want to take advantage." Jace kept his smile in check, but it was obvious he thought he was putting one over on me, uh, Rose.

I snorted. "You don't seem the type to worry about a woman's virtue." I really had no idea what scripted-Rose had suggested, and hoped I wasn't truly placing my body at risk.

"This won't be no penny ante like you're used to playing in your fancy parlors with your lady friends. I'll be happy to win your ranch off ya. Save me the passel of time and trouble I had planned at any rate." Jace's cruel smile returned, and he looked like a kid who'd been given free rein in a candy store.

So, Rose suggested a card game. What an idiot.

"There's a room behind the bar at the Yellow Star, where I've been doing business. Be there in two days' time at four in the afternoon. Go up to the bar and ask the barkeep if he has any tequila from South America. He'll direct you to the game. Tell no one. If I catch wind of the sheriff or that nosy ranger snooping around, they're dead." Jace gave me one last hard look before spinning and stalking to his horse. He climbed on and turned his mount to leave, tipping his hat. "See you soon, darlin'."

I gave him a finger pistol and winked. "Not if I see you first." My clever response was totally wasted on Jace, but it made me feel better. The heroine had just talked her way into hot water. I *hated* it when characters did that. Unfortunately, in this case, I couldn't stop reading or skip ahead.

****

It didn't take a genius to figure out where Jace Cutter would be. Even the sheriff figured it out on his own. He secured the bad guys for later retrieval, and we took off toward Mabel's, er, Rose's ranch.

I hated not knowing what lay ahead. Would the whole place be on fire? Would he hurt Mabel? No. The magic wouldn't do that. Kidnap, maybe, but she'd be okay. She had a gun and brown and black belts in various martial arts. I should be more concerned about Cutter.

We tore into the dooryard to find Mabel trying to play fetch with Scamp using a balled-up sock.

"Thank goodness! I am so bored." She tucked the ball into a pocket and dusted off her skirts. "What's going on? You guys are riding like there's a fire." She glanced at the barn and gave us a half smile. "I guess I can't blame you."

Beau swung down from his horse and walked to Mabel. He grasped her hand in his. "I was worried. We caught some of Cutter's gang today, but not the man himself. Did he come here?"

Mabel looked over Beau's shoulder at me. "He came by, and I think Rose offered to bet her ranch in a game of cards with him in two days."

"Man, she's dumb!" I climbed down and knocked my dusty hat against my thigh.

"That's what I said! I am totally chunking this book when we get back." She refocused on Beau, who'd started talking.

"…he's going to be, we can make a plan. I don't like the idea of using you as bait." Beau frowned.

I joined them, listening closely to Beau's great plan so I'd know where to be and when. The magic was great about getting us into position, but I'd rather manage it on my own. I looked at Mabel. "He's right. I don't like using you as bait either."

Mabel shrugged. "It's not like we have any other options. It'll be fine. The sooner we get it done, the sooner we can go home. Who knows, maybe it will present the right set of circumstances for Beau to self-realize."

"Maybe." The sheriff didn't strike me as the sharpest crayon in the box. I'd hedge my bets. I tuned back in to the sheriff's rambling.

"…will take position in one of the storefronts across from the saloon while I cover the back."

"It barely sounds like I'm needed." Further proof I wasn't the hero. "I thought the ranger was hot on the trail of this guy. I'm supposed to let the local yokel bring him in?" I shouldn't let myself get irritated about it.

"I don't know, Sam. Just because we're making this plan, doesn't mean it will *go* as planned. Something will go wrong. Plot twist!" She smiled and squeezed my arm.

"Why are you so excited about it?"

"Because Beau will have to save me somehow. It'll be super-romantic. He'll look into my eyes and realize who he is. I'm just anxious. I don't want to wait two whole days." Mabel's body hummed with excitement as she leaned toward the sheriff.

I loved Mabel and wanted her to be happy. If she couldn't be happy with me, why couldn't the magic at least find her someone better than this clown?

Chapter 13

The Happiest Girl in the West
Love's Gamble
*Cliff stirred. Rose's small hand rested on his chest
as if it belonged there. As far as he was concerned, it did.
But a wandering Texas Ranger couldn't compete with an
upstanding town sheriff. The best Cliff could do was
catch Jace Cutter so Rose could run her ranch in peace.*

*The day dawned bright and new, in direct opposition
to the dirty business ahead of them that morning. No
matter what happened, nothing was more important than
keeping Rose safe, even if she wasn't to be his in the end.*

My eyelids flew open, and I flinched. Mabel's hand
rested on my chest, just like in the bizarre dream.

She rolled away at the disruption and mumbled,
"What?"

"Nothing. We've been here too long. I'm starting to
dream in narration. Go back to sleep."

She didn't respond. I wouldn't be able to fall back
asleep with the sun streaming in, and the possibility of
having another dream made me afraid to anyway. This
may be our last night in-book. I regretted sleeping
through Mabel being snuggled up next to me. My left
side cooled as the warmth from her body faded.

With Mabel returned to unconsciousness, I quickly
switched my long johns for my jeans. My shirt supply
was running low, the reason I'd slept without one, but

there should be two or three left by my count. I didn't have a plan for running out. I'm not sure where I'd pin my ranger badge.

A pile of women's clothing draped the bureau. That was new. I pulled open the bottom drawer, where my shirts should have been, to find only one remaining. I pulled it out and shrugged it on or tried to. It was tight. Too tight. Like cowboy stripper tight, or so I assumed.

I removed it and tossed it on the bed. The middle and top drawers revealed more women's clothing. "What the heck?" I grumbled, picking up the offending article again.

The too tight shirt was spaghetti western ugly in cream-colored fabric worn so thin you could nearly read newsprint through it. The front and back yokes, button placket, and cuffs were accented with brown piping. Decorative curls were stitched across the shoulders and upper back. The collar came to sharp points on each side.

Garbled mumbling came from the bed. I sighed and slipped the shirt back on. The arms fit, sort of, but the cuffs strangled my wrists when buttoned. I had no range of motion through my shoulders and arms, and I heard stitches pop every time I stretched or flexed. Buttoning the top two front buttons was out of the question and the tails stayed tucked into my pants so long as I didn't think about raising my arms.

Resigned to a shirt better befitting my fourteen-year-old self, I put on my boots and went to see about breakfast.

****

I nestled my burning face deeper into the blankets. Why did I keep gravitating toward Sam in my sleep and how could such a hard chest be so comfortable?

Thankfully Sam thought the move was unconscious on my part. I didn't need embarrassing complications with my friend today.

As soon as he left the room, I rose to sort out my own wardrobe. Skirts were piled on the dresser. I fingered the shiny fabric on top. The pearl brocade wouldn't have been my first choice, but I couldn't deny it was much nicer than the cotton calicos I'd been wearing. The magic supplied me with a love declaration outfit.

In addition to the brocade, the pile included three more underskirts and a pair of pantaloons. The dresser drawers provided a pearl-button blouse and a puffy-sleeved jacket matching the top skirt. A pair of new heeled boots sat in place of the worn pair I left there the night before.

With the marred dresser mirror to guide me, I twisted my hair into a low bun, wishing I knew how to accomplish a fancier updo to compliment my outfit. Once everything was in place, I joined Sam in the kitchen.

"I think that's yours." Sam used a spatula to point toward a kitchen chair.

A creamy white hat hung from the back. The ribbon around the band matched my dress and the bow tails hung several inches below the brim. Fluffy ostrich feathers stuck out of the bow's center.

I picked it up, pulled out a long wooden skewer, and placed it on my head. "It even matches my dress. Is this right?" I modeled for Sam.

He set the spatula down and made an adjustment to the hat. "Pins?" He held out a hand.

"Just this one." I handed him the hat pin.

He studied it a moment then jabbed it through a spot in the back, anchoring it to my head. He stood back. "You look nice. Pretty."

I twirled. "Thank you. The magic left it for me. Today must be the day."

Sam shook his head. "For what?"

"For Beau to self-realize and declare his love, of course." I wandered to the stove to see what Sam made for breakfast. He followed.

"I hope you're right. I'm ready to go home. Besides, this is the last of the food. Sit down, and I'll fix you a plate. You don't want to get bacon grease on your outfit."

After placing a plate in front of me, Sam joined me at the table. He didn't look at me or say much, forcing me to carry the conversation.

"Do you remember what you're supposed to do today?"

He fixed me with a glare. "I'm not a moron. I can sit in a shop and watch the front of the saloon while Sheriff Toothsome saves the day."

I smiled. "You and your fancy words. Beau does have nice teeth, though, doesn't he?"

Sam rolled his eyes. "It means attractive. More so if his mouth is closed, in my opinion."

"Why are you being so hateful? I thought you'd be happy for me. No more crying on your shoulder when the wrong guys dump me, because Beau is the *right* guy. Always and forever. My happily ever after."

He sighed and rubbed a hand down his face. "You're right. I'm sorry, Mabes. I'm just tired and taking it out on you. Why don't you go see what the horse situation is for this morning, and I'll clean up breakfast."

Dabbing a cloth napkin to my lips, I rose and circled

the table to Sam. He eyed me warily as I leaned down and wrapped my arms around his shoulders. Despite the harsh conditions and bathing situation, Sam's own comforting scent greeted me. I kissed his cheek and whispered in his ear, "Be happy for me."

Sam relaxed into me for a moment before pulling away. "I am. I only want you to be happy."

Searching his gaze, I saw only truth. Satisfied, I released him and headed to the barn. With Sam's smell clinging to me from the hug, reservations crept in. Would I ever be comfortable enough with Beau to be both friends and lovers? What would happen to my relationship with Sam? He'd never failed me, and I wasn't ignorant of how he'd allowed me to take advantage of his kind heart over the years.

I crossed the yard to where Bertie and another horse were harnessed to the wagon. Sam's horse munched grass nearby. I stumbled, as if tripped up by an unpleasant realization. What *did* Sam get out of our relationship? Sure, we played together as children, but as we got older, it was Sam being there for me. My breakups, my heartache, my spiraling devastation. Shame burned through me. I was a horrible friend. Sam should be glad to be done with me. I'd be part of a couple. He'd no longer have to pretend to like me for the sake of our families. Our friendship could just fade away.

I rubbed the horse's nose to calm myself. "What am I going to do, Bertie?" I was so wrapped in my thoughts; I didn't hear Sam's approach until he spoke.

"Why'd you name your horse after your sister?" He stood there in his well-worn jeans and ridiculously tight shirt.

"Sometimes Bertie's a good listener and sometimes

she's a horse's ass. It seemed fitting." I shrugged.

Sam laughed. "I'll tell her you said so."

His lightened mood helped me set aside my turmoil. "Oh, she knows."

He held his hand out for me. "Looks like everything's ready. Let me help you up."

After a couple false starts, Sam simply picked me up by my waist and placed me in the wagon, cursing under his breath at the sound of threads breaking. His muscles weren't just for show. All my skirts probably added a good twenty pounds.

"Onward to destiny!" I called, flicking the reins.

Sam's horse fell in beside the wagon. "That was incredibly corny."

I tilted my nose in the air. "Do you have a better battle cry?"

He chuckled wryly. "Is that what it was supposed to be?" He thought for a moment, then raised a fist. "To destiny and beyond!"

"You did not just misquote Buzz Lightyear to me." A laugh bubbled to the surface, but I maintained my incredulous expression.

"Never!" His smile softened. "How's this: Strength of heart and strength of friends, betwixt the two the future wends."

My heart melted a little. Someone who wanted to be rid of me wouldn't say something like that. "Aww. That's sweet, Sam. It sounds more like a toast. What's it from?"

He shrugged and avoided my gaze. "I don't recall. It seemed appropriate." His eyes finally met mine. "No matter what happens today, I'll always be there for you."

I nodded at his solemn promise. There was nothing left to say or do but to go meet my destiny.

Chapter 14

Reunion
Love's Gamble

This time when we arrived in town, both Mabel's wagon and my horse headed to the sheriff's office. I kept waiting for something to happen, something to prevent us from going forward with the sheriff's ridiculously unsafe plan. I held out hope until my horse parked itself at the sheriff's hitching post.

I climbed down from my horse and went to assist Mabel. "It's not too late to back out."

"Sam, we can be done with this before the sun sets and go home for real showers and food. Why would I want to back out?" Mabel hitched up her skirts and hopped to the ground.

"For the record, I don't like it."

She walked past me to the office door. "Noted."

I reached around her and pulled open the door, allowing her to enter first. Beau sat behind his desk. His face brightened when he spotted Mabel.

"Good afternoon, Rose. Ranger. I have a deputy keeping an eye out. He'll let us know when Cutter arrives at the saloon." He stood and came around the desk to take Mabel's hand. "I wouldn't ask this of you if there was any other way. But, even still, you can say no. We can bring him in based on the suspicions listed on his wanted poster. But without catching him in the act, a judge could cut him loose."

Mabel patted his hand. "It's sweet of you to be concerned, but I want to help. I knew this would be the best chance to move our relationship forward. No matter what happens, I know I can count on you to keep me safe."

I rolled my eyes at Mabel's attempt to drag Beau off-script.

Beau smiled. "I knew you'd say that. You're my brave girl."

And now I'm throwing up a little in my mouth.

Beau looked at me. "You'll stand watch in the apothecary across the street. I've already alerted Mr. Smickle. He'll close up as soon as you're in position and clear out. I doubt Cutter will exit out the front, but I want all our bases covered."

I nodded. What else could I do, tell him his plan had more holes than a sieve? Maybe I could point out that Rose participating in this charade was unnecessary. The fact that Cutter's face graced a wanted poster, and he had a Texas Ranger on his tail was enough reason to bring him in. In the wild west, the burden of proof was on the accused.

Pulling a pocket watch out of his coat, the sheriff glanced at the time. "Shouldn't be long now. The card game is scheduled for thirty minutes from now. Cutter will arrive just before."

The office door flew open and banged against the wall. "Sheriff, sheriff, come quick!"

If this was the deputy, the minimum law enforcement age was younger than I thought.

Beau finally let go of Mabel and put both hands on

the boy's shoulders. "Slow down, Timmy. Where are your folks?" He glanced over the boy toward the door.

"That's what I'm tryin' to tell ya. A bad man came and tied 'em up the other day. I hid behind the barn, waitin' for a chance to save 'em, but he never left. I finally decided to run to town to git ya. I was almost here when I saw the bad man on his horse. I was afeared he was a comin' for me, but he went to the saloon." The boy panted and swiped an arm across his tear-streaked face.

The sheriff turned to me. "Timmy's family is homesteading in a dugout near where we nabbed Cutter's gang the other day."

My body stiffened. "Don't do it. Don't send me on a fool's errand. The boy can go back and untie them now that Cutter is here. I'm not leaving Mabel in town alone."

"I agree. Having the family's testimony against Cutter would be added ammunition in the case against him. He usually doesn't leave loose ends like that lying around. We need to make sure they're protected." Beau tapped his chin in thought.

"You know that's not what I said, you moron."

"Sam, be nice. Follow the script." Mabel glared at me and stomped her foot.

Beau patted me on the back, nearly knocking me over. "Godspeed, Ranger. Timmy can show you the way. I'll make sure Rose is safe."

Timmy took my hand and stared up at me with his dirty face and pleading eyes. He was convincing for a scripted character. Not that I'd let that sway me. Mabel on the other hand…

"This is the way the story is supposed to go. Your presence will not make anything happen differently. If anything, this guarantees Beau is the one to rescue me."

Mabel's imploring look didn't convince me so much as remind me that if I stuck around, I'd have to witness her and Beau's sickening love fest.

"I'll go. I don't like it, though. Do one thing for me, please."

Mabel nodded.

I stepped over to where she stood. "Proceed with caution. Don't count on the magic to keep you safe. If guns come out, hit the floor. If Cutter touches you, use your martial arts training."

She nodded again. "Thank you, Sam, for everything." She wrapped her arms around me and half a second later, I returned her embrace, maybe for the last time. Several popping sounds came from the vicinity of my shoulders.

"That shirt!" Mabel giggled and drew away. "Go on. Go save that family Ranger McGrath."

****

I galloped across the prairie with little Timmy tucked in front of me. Nothing looked familiar but the horse seemed to know the way. A small barn appeared in the distance. Timmy pointed at it, but I didn't see the kid's house.

As we rounded the hill, a door and windows built into the back side came into view. A dugout. Literally, a home dug out of the side of a hill. I should have expected as much.

Tim scrambled down from my horse without assistance. "This way, Ranger."

I followed the kid into the house. He crossed the room and began assisting the couple sitting on the floor, already working on their bonds. The only light came from the west-facing windows, throwing the room into shadows. The man freed a hand and stood before turning to finish freeing the woman. Their clothes were baggy and workworn, but I'd recognize the man's shaggy blond hair and the woman's glasses anywhere.

"Were you afraid you were missing out on the action?" I asked.

"Sam!" My mom ran over and wrapped me in a hug. I saw my parents every couple weeks or so, but after spending time in the book, it felt like a year.

My dad joined in and wrapped us both in a bear hug. "I can't wait to hear how you got into this mess, son."

Like Mabel's parents, Peter and Bobbie Celansky were well-versed in book craziness. They'd purposely gone into books with Aunt Penny and Uncle Tripp, though their adventures were tame compared to what Mabel and I were experiencing. I hoped they could give better intel than Mabel's parents who hadn't had a clue and only wanted to dance. My mom probably knew more about all the magic rules than Aunt Penny; she's the one who wrote them all down.

"I'll tell you about it, but I need to pick your brain for some advice."

My dad thumbed a finger over his shoulder. "You can start by explaining who this kid is and why he keeps calling me Pa."

Chapter 15

Anyone for Go Fish?
Love's Gamble

Recalling Jace's threat, I wondered if Beau or Sam risked true danger in this scheme.

"It's time to go, Rose. Cutter shouldn't see you coming from my office. We'll go out to the alley, and you can enter through the back of the mercantile. From there, go directly to the Yellow Star. I'll already be in place by the back entrance." Beau offered her his arm.

She placed her hand there. "Are you sure you'll be safe? Jace threatened—"

"That's awful sweet of you, darlin'. I'm a professional, perfectly capable of keeping myself and you from harm." He turned and took both of my hands in his. "When this is all over, I have something important to ask you."

Who did, Beau or my soul mate? "I can't wait." I tilted my chin up in invitation.

Beau lowered his lips to mine. They were soft but dry. He applied the perfect amount of pressure and moved them over mine with perfect mastery. It was one of the technically better kisses I'd ever received, and that's saying a lot. But something was missing.

He pulled away, eyes sliding open. "Let's go, darlin'."

As he escorted me through the alley, I mulled over

the kiss. It ticked all the boxes but didn't make my heart flip. We passed behind the diner. Waste bins overflowed and flies buzzed lazily. That was it!

My first impression was that Beau didn't smell like Sam. I couldn't smell the hint of detergent on his clothes or the faint whiff of chlorine that always clung to his hair and skin. What my mind hadn't grasped until just now, was that Beau didn't smell like anything. The stench from those trash bins should have knocked me sideways, but nothing. They didn't smell because they weren't written to. Just like Beau.

Instead of flipping, my heart flopped to the bottom of my chest with a dull thud. Beau didn't have a scent because the author neglected to give him one. Only real people had body odor. I glanced at my handsome escort. He couldn't be my soul mate. He didn't have a soul, or heart, or even his own opinion.

Now what? Did my guy just fail to show up? Was it Jace Cutter? He did appear early on, and he was too handsome for a villain. Beau pulled me to a stop.

"This is where I leave you. Go inside and wait about ten minutes before heading over. That will put you there about five minutes before the appointed time." He leaned down and kissed me on the cheek. "Be careful, sweet Rose. I'll be nearby."

I didn't know what to say, still reeling from my mind-blowing epiphany. I entered through the back door of the mercantile as planned. An old woman sat scooping dry beans from a barrel into a burlap sack. She nodded as I passed without pausing her task.

"Miz Rose." A grizzled man behind the counter acknowledged me as he finished with a customer.

I wandered the aisles, temporarily distracted with

the oddities people actually paid money for in the olden days. One whole shelf held tins, bottles, and jars. The term snake oil salesman readily jumped to mind. The variety and outlandishness of the toiletries made me wonder what passed for grooming among the townsfolk.

New willow brooms sat in a barrel in a corner and bolts of calico and muslin were stacked on the back wall. I was admiring the spools of lace and ribbon when a tap on my shoulder nearly caused me to jump out of my skin.

"It's time, Miz Rose. The sheriff told me earlier to help ya know when to go." The shopkeeper turned and shuffled back to the counter.

I took a deep breath. Instead of gawking around the store like a country bumpkin I should have been making a plan to deal with Jace. The worst thing that could happen is we get to the end of the book with no one self-realizing. It would suck a lot. I'd have to do this all over again with a new book and I couldn't in good conscience ask Sam to go with me. Not after this fiasco.

Operation Woo Jace Cutter was a go. I stuck my head out the door, looking for the Yellow Star. I spotted the apothecary shop, where Sam was originally supposed to wait, kitty corner from the mercantile. The Yellow Star was right next door to my position.

I walked over and pushed my way through the batwing doors. Men sat at the bar drinking and most of the tables were occupied by card players. A man wearing suspenders pounded out a ditty on an upright piano while barmaids in lowcut gowns worked the room. I made my way to the bar.

I leaned toward the barkeep, careful not to let my clothes touch the sticky bar top. "Do you have any tequila from South America?"

The man paused wiping a beer mug and took my measure. "I have one, Miss, but are you absolutely sure you want to try it? It packs a wallop and could be mighty dangerous for a little thing like you."

"I'm sure."

He jerked his head to the side, indicating I should follow. I rounded the bar and trailed the man down a short hall only accessible from behind the counter. He came to a door and tapped out a pattern on the wood paneling. It sounded like *shave and a haircut*.

The door opened a crack to expose a short man with an over-waxed mustache and greasy hair. He looked from the barkeep to me, then opened the door wide enough so I could slip through, but not so wide I could do it without sliding against him. Eww.

The door clicked shut behind me. Jace was the room's only other occupant.

"Rose, I wasn't sure you'd come." Jace rose from his seat and pulled a chair out for me.

As I sat, I took in the room. The creepy man stood in front of the door, the only exit. The interior room had no windows and only the table and four chairs for furniture. It still felt stuffy and cramped. Cigar smoke clung to the ceiling in a stagnant cloud.

"Why wouldn't I? I want you out of town and out of my life. This seemed the easiest way to accomplish that."

"It's adorable that you think it will play out that way. I'm looking forward to winning your ranch fair and square. I'll even give you twenty-four hours to pack your things because I'm a generous guy." He pushed her chair in, then reclaimed the seat across from her. "Would you like some refreshment?"

"I'd kill for a strawberry margarita. I don't even care

where the tequila came from." A girl could hope.

Jace nodded. "Very well then, we'll begin. I assume faro is acceptable?" He raised an eyebrow at me. "Or we could play brag or monte if you'd rather."

I assessed my opponent and potential soul mate. It was difficult to imagine him as a regular guy while he acted so slimy. I tried to unobtrusively smell him when he pushed in my chair, but the lingering odors of beer, cigar, and B.O. in the room made it difficult to scent anything else.

Rakish good looks and rock star blond hair marked him as a bad boy, one of my favorite types, but that didn't mean he was in the real world. For all I know, real world Jace could be an investment banker or gas station night manager.

I'd never preferred mustaches on my dates. They made guys look a little seedy for some reason. Beards, like Sam's, gave off a lumberjack vibe I'd started to appreciate. But again, real world Jace might not wear one. Getting him to self-realize was key.

"Can we play *Go Fish*?" I asked hopefully.

"Faro it is. Good choice." Jace began dealing laying cards face-up on the table while I grumbled to myself about lack of choice in refreshment *and* game. I'd have to leave a review. One-star establishment. Do not recommend.

"Farnsworth, come serve as dealer."

The creepy doorman accepted the deck from Jace. He shuffled the deck once and lifted the top card, showed it to us, queen of hearts, then placed it face-up on the table.

Jace picked up two chips, red and blue, from the pile next to his ashtray. I hoped real-Jace wasn't a smoker.

He placed the chips on the face-up ace and the seven in front of us. I took two red chips from the pile at my elbow and placed them on the four and king. This was unlike anything I'd ever played, even online solitaire.

Farnsworth drew two cards from his deck and laid them down, first an ace then a king. He frowned and removed Jace's blue chip from the ace and put it in the dealer pile. He took a red chip from his pile and placed it with mine on the king. This seemed like a good sign.

Jace scowled—definitely a good sign—and moved his red chip to the queen. He added a red chip to the ace. I took the red chip from the dealer and started a new winnings pile, then moved my remaining red chips to different cards, too.

Play continued, each of us winning and losing chips to the dealer. Just when I thought I had a fair handle on the rules, Jace added a penny to one of his chips. I decided not to muddy the waters by adding real coin to the mix.

"Last three, boss." He raised his eyebrows nervously.

"Looks like I'm ahead, Rose, but you have this one last round to redeem yourself." Jace chuckled. "I think three, then seven, and a Jack for last card." He turned his gaze to Rose.

I'd been keeping up merely by chance until this point. It was easy to forget the outcome had already been decided, I just wasn't privy to what it was. The magic had done a good job of making me feel like I'd been making my own choices the entire game. Now it looked like Jace wanted me to bet on the order of the last three cards.

I glanced over at all the pairs already played. Jace

must have been counting cards the whole game to be confident on which three remained. He didn't have any way of knowing the order unless he cheated.

Jace placed a small stack of chips in front of the dealer. "Your turn, Rose." He smirked.

I took a deep breath then expelled it. "Jack first, then three and seven." I pushed my entire pile of winnings plus all the chips at my elbow toward Farnsworth. A bead of sweat rolled down his temple. He pinched the corner of the second card in the remaining deck.

I slammed my hand on top of his and the cards. "From the top, if you please."

His eyes cut to Jace, but I didn't dare divert my focus. I slowly moved my hand away. He flipped the first card. "Jack." The second. "Three." The third. "Seven."

Jace's chair scraped back from the table. "Not possible. You cheated. I'll not honor it,"

I laughed. "It looked to me like you were trying to cheat. Don't dis my superior card playing and random luck."

Jace came around the table at me, his lips pressed thin with grim intent. "Looks like we'll have to go to plan B, Farnsworth."

"Beau!" I yelled once before Jace's hand clamped over my mouth.

Farnsworth moved in and pressed my wrists together before deftly wrapping them with rope. Jace removed his hand long enough to stuff a—please let it be clean—bandana in my mouth. Before I could spit it out, he wrapped another one around my head to hold it in.

I concentrated on not hyperventilating. This was scripted. The magic won't hurt me. Right?

Chapter 16

The Lone POV
Love's Gamble

My parents caught up pretty quick, being already familiar with the Kinney family brand of crazy. My mom's wheels were turning while my dad tried to play with Timmy. He finally took him out to the barn, which seemed to be scripted, and Mom and I were left alone.

"Did your aunt Penny say anything to help you two?"

"Not really. She and Uncle Tripp danced most of the time."

Mom's lips turned up in an indulgent grin. "I'm sure they did. Good for them." She pushed her glasses up on her nose and crinkled her brow. "But that doesn't help you and Mabel. You said she's in town at a card game?"

I told her how the plot had progressed thus far and Mabel's relationship with Beau. I explained how my character was the foil and my proximity to Rose would incite action on his part. Action most likely happening in town as we spoke.

"And how did you come to this conclusion, Son?"

It never turned out well for me when Mom called me 'Son.' "All my major interactions occurred in the presence of Mabel or Beau. Therefore, all the action happened during one of their POVs." I turned this information over in my head, sure of the accuracy of my findings.

"And remind me again why your dad and I put so much money into your *English Literature* education." Hands on hips, she gave me a probing look. I had missed something important.

"The sheriff is Mabel's soul mate," I said with confidence I no longer felt.

Mom continued to glare.

"The sheriff isn't Mabel's soul mate? Then why does he have a POV?" I tried to rearrange the new facts to fit into the narrative when Mom interrupted me.

"Let's start back at the beginning. Walk me through it." At least she'd stopped glaring.

"I staggered up to Mabel's porch and knocked on the door. My horse, gun—"

Mom waved away my words. "No. The beginning. Before you were in the book."

Oh. "Mabel had been dumped again—"

"Good. I hated that guy. Continue."

"She called me like she always does. I brought her ice cream. We were sitting on the couch. I teased her about the book she was reading."

"So Mabel was reading a book while you were there?"

I shook my head. "No, it was lying on her coffee table. She told me Aunt Penny had shared more about the family legacy book thing and that it was true. I didn't believe her. The book was a cheesy western romance." I glanced around the room. "*This* cheesy western romance, with a shirtless dude on the cover."

"And Mabel took the book and inadvertently read you both in?"

Again, I shook my head. "I grabbed the book and held it out of her reach. Then I opened it to her marked page…and started reading." The ramifications hit me like a freight train, or, under the circumstances, a steam locomotive while Mom smiled like a Cheshire cat. "Mom? What does this mean?"

She lovingly smacked me upside the head. "You know exactly what this means. Is this, right now, not a major event in your POV? The only people able to read into the books are the legacy heir and her soul mate. You may not have been aware of that technicality."

Mabel only saw me as a brother, though. Something wasn't right. And then there was Beau. "The magic has been acting wonky the whole time. Like maybe it's expired or gone toxic or something. We haven't been able to leave the story. And it does weird things."

Mom smiled. "The magic was wonky in the last book your aunt Penny read into, but it was mostly my fault. What is it doing to you?"

"Not that I'm complaining, but it's making sure we're fed. And my shirts keep disappearing. Yesterday I had a drawer full and this morning this was the only one left." I spread my arms open so she could see how badly it fit. A button popped from the strain and rolled across the floor.

She watched it roll into the shadows. "You say there was a shirtless cowboy on the cover?"

"Yes," I grumbled.

A laugh burst from her lips. "Sam, you remind me so much of your father sometimes. *You* are the shirtless cowboy. The magic is simply contriving to keep you shirtless. Sweetheart," she brushed the hair away from my brow and ran her fingers over my beard. "You and

Mabel are soul mates. Your aunt Penny and I always hoped as much but had given up since you two turned out so different. But in almost three hundred years, the magic has never been wrong."

Elation filled me, immediately followed by dread. "I'm the hero. I have to go!"

Chapter 17

Awry
Love's Gamble

I kept the panic at bay, knowing Beau waited at the back door. He wouldn't let Jace take me out of the saloon. I recalled Mom telling me about Uncle Gregorio accidentally attacking her when he was in character as the villain. All it took to break him out of character was my mom saying his name. But I didn't know Jace's real name. And I couldn't talk. I needed to come up with a solution I could work with.

Farnsworth opened the door so Jace could drag me out. I thrashed and kicked and attempted to brace my legs around the door frame. Anything to prevent him from taking me. Farnsworth stepped clear of my flying feet and removed a gun from his waistband. I stilled, my legs dropping, and allowed Jace to drag me out the door and up the hall.

We emerged behind the bar. With all the people in the saloon, someone would help me. The barkeep averted his eyes and walked to the other end of the bar. Traitor. The piano music stopped abruptly. but no one moved a muscle. Whether due to fear or apathy, there'd be no help from the saloon patrons.

Instead of turning down the hall leading to the back door, Jace headed for the batwing doors. I renewed my struggling. He looked back at Farnsworth and jerked his head toward the street. Farnsworth ran ahead of us, and I changed tactics. I let my whole body go limp, becoming dead weight.

"Finally," Jace murmured as he hoisted me onto his shoulder in a fireman's carry. His muscular arm pinned my legs together, immobilizing me. All I could do was flop like a fish on his shoulder, which I attempted, only to discover I didn't have the abdominal strength to do it for very long. Randomly, I thought to be impressed with Sam's hat-pinning skills. My hair felt more likely to come out at the roots before my thrashing would dislodge the hat.

Jace strode through the doors. I had to tuck my head to keep from getting smacked in the face when he stopped just outside them. The other unfortunate result of my position was the inability to see in front of us.

"Good job, Kendrick. I'll take it from here. Keep an eye out for the sheriff and that ranger. Make sure they don't follow us.

On top of the regular town noises, I picked out the sound of horses nearby. Kendrick must be another minion. What did he do to deserve thanks? I heard the squeak of wood and leather, then boots hitting the boardwalk next to us.

"All yours, boss," the new voice, presumably Kendrick, said.

I heard the rattle and squeak of a cheap door opening before being unceremoniously dumped on the floor. *A stagecoach? This is terrible writing. I read enough of these types of books to know it takes more than one minion to rob, let alone steal a stagecoach.*

The door slammed shut behind me and I heard someone, probably Jace, climb up to the driver's seat. I was beginning to reconsider his potential as my soul mate. He'd have to do a lot of groveling to get back in my good graces.

"Yah!" The coach lurched forward, and I discovered there are more uncomfortable positions to be in than draped over someone's shoulder.

****

I approached town with the same eerie feeling as the first time Mabel and I visited. No wagons came or went to hint at the hustle and bustle happening within the town's boundaries. Almost there. I saw the people and horses moving about. I turned my head when my peripheral caught a stagecoach leaving town at the far end.

Remembering my conversation with Mabel that first day, I was tempted to stop and watch it. Would it continue on to the horizon or disappear in a few hundred feet when the road ran out? It was a question for another day. I needed to find Mabel and didn't slow my horse's pace as I charged into town.

A crowd gathered in front of the saloon. I couldn't spot the sheriff, Mabel, or Jace. It didn't bode well. I jumped from my mount to the sound of several more popped shirt seams. A man with a deputy star held a short, mustached man while a man wearing an apron helped the sheriff to his feet. A third man lay unconscious on the boardwalk. The crowd parted for me.

"What happened? Where's Mabel?" I demanded.

"I got one, but the other jumped me." Beau rubbed the back of his head.

"Where's Mabel?" I growled.

"I don't know where they're headed. But we should easily be able to catch up with the stage." He turned to the deputy. "Lock these two up."

The stage. The one leaving town moments ago. I wasn't violent by nature, but I'd never wanted to hit a man as badly as I wanted to hit Beau Wilson. The man had one job. I paused and my mind instantly re-slotted all the facts. Dammit. I have one job. Mabel is mine to rescue. Mabel is mine.

A grin spread across my face as I mounted my horse. The sheriff's horse conveniently sidled up next to me. It looked like I'd have company.

"Let's go!" Beau called as he leapt to his horse.

I didn't need to be told twice. I followed the path of the stagecoach, glad my fictional horse didn't need a breather after our ride into town. The taller buildings gave way to less substantial structures and we finally emerged from the town proper. The stage had disappeared; I'd have to let Beau take the lead.

I followed, and though the road dissipated, wheel tracks continued on, leading into low hills. Beau pulled to a stop when we crested the first one. He pointed at a tiny stagecoach in the distance. It could not have realistically outpaced us to that extent in the short amount of time before we took up pursuit. Fictionally, yes. Realistically, no. It was frustrating not being able to depend on simple laws of nature and physics.

We pressed on. The stage appeared closer when we topped the next rise. A body of water sparkled in the distance.

"He's heading to Lake Saddleback. The surrounding area is riddled with caves. We need to close the distance." Beau spurred his horse on.

Losing sight of our quarry, we started down the hill. I wished I could speed up the chase somehow. My anxiety grew every time the stage disappeared from view. When they came into view again, the stage was within five hundred yards of the lake. Soon it would have to veer right toward the foothills and aforementioned caves.

But Cutter didn't turn. He drew close to the lake, then swung the coach in a wide circle so it faced back the way it came. The stagecoach stopped and Cutter climbed down just as we lost sight of them again.

Time seemed to slow. My horse couldn't go any faster. One terrifying scenario after another flew through my head. Was Cutter going to make a final stand? Would he hold Mabel hostage at gunpoint? Will they have already escaped into the vast cave system by the time we reached the lake? Or something worse?

To my horror, the sight greeting us was Cutter galloping away on one of the four unharnessed stage horses and the coach rolling backwards into the lake.

Chapter 18

Hot Pursuit
Love's Gamble

"I've got a bone to pick with Cutter. You go after Rose!" Beau yelled before angling away to intercept the antagonist.

The minute the rolling stage came into view, I had forgotten Jace Cutter. Now Beau was out of the way, too. Good riddance. I just hoped Mabel's rescue didn't turn out to be a two-man job.

My shirttails flapped in the wind as I raced down the hill. The restricted movement and general annoyance of the too-small shirt had plagued me all day. I yanked at the placket, sending the remaining buttons flying, then ripped away the fasteners at the cuffs with a tug to each. "I can't believe I'm taking my shirt off on purpose." *I can't believe I'm talking out loud to myself.*

I flung the offending material away and reached for my right boot. Removing it proved especially challenging at the speed we traveled, but I intended to ride my horse into the lake as far as I could before swimming.

Glancing ahead, I estimated about three quarters of a mile, maybe less, remained between me and the lake. The water had reached the coach windows and flowed in, speeding the rate of immersion. Why hadn't Mabel tried to get out? It didn't bear thinking on. I only hoped she had climbed to the seat and wasn't unconscious on the floor.

I freed my boot and tossed it aside before bending to struggle with my left one. It came loose and I dropped it as my horse splashed into the water. The coach had rolled about twenty-five feet into the lake. The water rose to four inches below the top of the window. There would still be a pocket of air at the top.

My horse balked when it got breast-deep. Close enough. I climbed on top of the saddle and dove off, streamlining the remaining distance. Through the window, fabric floated and billowed. Mabel's dress. I couldn't make out her position.

I came up for air then dove under again, forcing my way through the open window. I collected cloth into my arms to keep from getting tangled. Relief filled me when I felt a deliberate tug in return.

Shoving the fabric beneath me, I swam to the top of the space.

"Sam!" Mabel sobbed. She stood on the bench seat in the highest corner, hands bound in front of her, feathered hat crushed against the ceiling. Water lapped at a bandana tied around her neck.

"It's okay. I'll get you out." I swam over and began tearing away her skirts.

"I couldn't get out, Sam. I couldn't tear them with my hands tied and they're too heavy," Mabel explained between panicked gasps.

"Shh. It's all over. I'll get you out." I couldn't do anything about her ropes without a knife. Poor planning on my part. I managed to strip her down to her bloomers but needed her calm before trying to escape.

"I just kept thinking, the magic won't hurt me, the

magic won't hurt me, but it really feels like the magic might be trying to kill me."

"No one is going to die, but you have to stay calm for me. Can you do that?" I grasped her shoulders and held her gaze, noticing she now angled her head to keep the water from her mouth. Time was running out.

She nodded.

"Wait here for just a second." I gathered an armload of the cloth floating around us. Ducking under the water, I maneuvered to the floor and crammed the offending flotsam under the bench. Hopefully, it would stay long enough for us to get out.

I broke the surface again. Relief flashed across Mabel's wet face. "We're going to take a deep breath. I'm going to back out and pull you by your hands," I explained as I pulled out the long pin and removed her ruined hat.

"What if I can't hold my breath as long as you?" Panic again tinted her voice.

I smiled, hoping to reassure her. "I doubt you could. But look," I glanced back at the door. "You can see that sliver of light because it's the surface of the lake. We're not all the way underwater yet, but we need to hurry. You only have to duck down long enough to get through the door, then I'll make sure to keep your head above water. I'm lifeguard trained, remember?"

She nodded again. Time to go.

"One, two, three." We both inhaled and dipped under the surface. Mabel immediately closed her eyes and thrust her hands in my direction. While I valued the trust she placed in me, I'd now have to pull her through the window like a lifeless carcass rather than a person who could avoid obstacles on her own.

113

I grabbed Mabel's hands with my left hand and used my right to help myself out the window. Once free, I pulled Mabel, guiding her head with my right hand. Once her shoulders and legs were free, I grabbed her waist and shoved her above water.

"Open your eyes. Anchor yourself to the roof with your hands while I figure out our next step." I floated her body closer to the sinking stagecoach.

She sucked in a breath of air and looped her bound hands over a brass finial on the top of the coach. "It's still sinking."

"Not very fast anymore. Just catch your breath for a second while I figure out the best way to get us to shore." I treaded water and assessed my surroundings. We were about fifty feet from shore, but the water was calm. Towing Mabel in wouldn't be an issue.

When I turned back to Mabel, her teeth were chattering. Shock? I hoped not. "Are you doing okay?"

"Yeah, just cold." Her blue tinted lips supported the statement.

"I don't think you'll be able to swim very efficiently in your bloomers and without use of your arms so I'm going to tow you in using a lifeguard technique." I wished like hell I could cut the ropes binding her hands. I wouldn't be able to undo the knot, wet as it was. Her wrists would be a mess by the time we got them undone.

I swam closer. "I'm going to get behind you and wrap my arm around you in a cross-chest tow carry. I'll side swim us in. It will be awkward, but easiest for you."

Mabel eyed me skeptically. "You tried that on me at the pool when I was twelve. We almost drowned."

I smiled. "I'm a better swimmer now and lifeguard trained. Trust me?"

She nodded and unhooked her bound hands from the stagecoach as I moved in behind her. Despite her chill, her body felt warm against my chest. I pulled her away from the stage and began paddling with one hand, her feet trailing behind.

"I think I can kick."

"No. Don't. You'll get in my way," I answered haltingly.

"I feel ridiculous."

"It's fine. Shh." I really couldn't carry on a conversation while swimming.

I hauled her in to where we could touch bottom and helped her to her feet. Exhausted, we waded to shore and collapsed on the grassy bank. My horse wandered over from where it had been grazing and stood over us.

"What does he want?" Mabel asked as she struggled into a seated position.

The horse nickered and turned his side toward us, exposing my saddlebag. I rose and scratched his neck. "What have you got for me, Lassie?" I unbuckled the bag and reached in. My fingers grasped the handle of a knife, which I pulled out.

"At least your horse remembered my suffering." Mabel held her bound hands up to me with a smirk.

"I just needed a few minutes to catch my breath after dragging your butt to shore." I carefully sliced through her bonds and returned the knife to the saddle bag.

Mabel shook out her hands to reestablish blood flow. I didn't see any blood, but her wrists were angry and red. Next, she smoothed her hands over her disheveled hair and squeezed the water out of the knotted length. She looked up at me.

"Sam, I don't know what to do now. Beau isn't my

destined true love. Then I thought it might be Jace, but obviously not."

I crouched down beside her and took her hands in mine. They were icy and her nail beds were tinged purple. I didn't know how to share what I'd learned. "What happened?"

"Beau never broke character, and he didn't even bother to rescue me. What was the magic thinking? I would have died if you hadn't come. What happened to you, anyway?"

My hands weren't much warmer, but I rubbed them over hers. The burden of the secret I had to tell her burned in my chest and up my neck. I'd be sweating before long.

"I followed the kid out to his family's dugout where Jace had tied up his parents. Only it turned out his parents were my parents."

Mabel frowned. "The ranger has parents? Unexpected plot twist."

"No, my *real* parents. I can't tell you what a relief it was to talk to my mom about all this."

She smiled and squirmed with anticipation. "That's awesome! What did she say? How do we get out of here? Where is my true love?"

It was now or never. "Mabes, do you remember how we got in here?"

"Of course. We were in my apartment and this book was on the coffee table." She looked at me like I was dense.

I sighed. "Mabel, think. I picked up your book. I started reading the chapter…I'm the one who's supposed to find my true love." I stared into her eyes, silently willing her to understand. I didn't expect the terror that flitted through them.

"No!"

Chapter 19

Connection in 5,4,3…
Love's Gamble
Sam's true love. It took a second to register. In that time, images of the girls dancing with Sam at the Grange Hall, the sisters with their parents leaving the hall, and the women who brought cookies after the fire flitted through my mind. I'd been so wrapped up in my own quest for true love, I'd barely paid attention to what Sam was up to when he wasn't with me. I'd ignored what was right in front of me. I couldn't lose Sam.

"No!" My stomach flipped over, and I felt like I was on my fourth tequila shot in the middle of airplane turbulence. The only thing grounding me was Sam's grip on my hands. I squeezed my eyes shut, willing myself not to vomit. Then, nothing. I cracked my eyelids open. Sam sat next to me on my sofa, looking a little green.

Home
He cleared his throat and released my hands. "You okay?"

I nodded mutely.

He stood and ran his hands over his shirtsleeves, then through his hair. Finally, he looked at me. "No?"

It took me a moment to catch up to speed. Right. The last thing I said before we came back, my selfish statement denying Sam future happiness after all the support he'd given me. My heart shattered in my chest. I had to be a good friend for once and be there for Sam. "I'm sorry—"

"You're sorry? It's all right, I get it. I'm just Sam, good enough to cry on and serve as your wingman, but that's it. I understand, I really do. I've wanted you forever. If you were ever going to feel anything for me, it would have happened by now. It's my own fault for carrying a torch all this time. The magic is just wrong." Sam's hands were clenched at his sides.

"What are you talking about?" What did I miss? "The other girls—"

"There are no other girls, Mabel! It's always been you." He grasped his shirt hem and pulled it off, revealing his glorious and once again clean-shaven chest. Turning, he pointed to the tattoo on his shoulder. "You, Mabes. My passion, my downfall. After every breakup with some stupid guy, I wonder, will she see me now? You refuse to see me, consider me." The beautifully inked artwork now seemed dark and bleak.

Realization settled and the shattered pieces of my heart trembled with hesitant hope. "Sam."

"I can't do it anymore. I'm done martyring myself. Don't call me." He pulled his shirt back on, briefly struggling with the wrong -side-out sleeves.

Shock kept me immobile.

Sam grabbed his jacket from the back of the chair, keys jingling in the pocket. I jumped when my apartment door slammed at his exit.

I slid to my back on the sofa. What had just happened? I eyed the piles of used tissue on my coffee table, tears and snot from another lifetime, it seemed. *Love's Gamble* lay discarded on the sofa next to my leg.

I nudged it and it fell to the floor with a clunk. *Stupid book*. Stupid magic. Stupid legacy. Tears threatened again. The magic wasn't wrong. I'd been wrong, apparently, for a very long time. I had to fix this.

****

I'd never before felt the need to text Sam with the frequency I did now. Before our book excursion, I'd contact him maybe once a week, and much more often after a breakup, to my chagrin.

The amount of time we'd recently spent together made his absence feel like I'd lost a limb. I wanted to laugh about how easy microwaves made life. I wanted to text him a picture of a cute dog I saw on my way to class. It looked like Scamp. I wanted a hug because I felt so bad and only Sam's arms would do.

I trudged home every day and moped. The ice cream Sam brought me that ill-fated night was long gone. I currently worked my way through a tube of chocolate chip cookie dough dipped in a can of funfetti frosting.

No matter how many times I caught my finger poised over Sam's face in my contacts, I restrained myself from calling or texting. He needed time, and I needed time to figure out how to fix things.

Sam and I are soul mates. I wish I could say I worked it out on my own. The morning after our return to normalcy, I called my mom to check in. She very patiently explained to her idiot daughter that, even though the magic was misbehaving, only the legacy heir (me) and her soul mate could read themselves into a plot.

I asked if there was any possibility one of the other girls in the story might be Sam's, praying all the while they weren't. Mom responded using short, simple words that I was the main character.

Aunt Bobbie called me, too. I almost didn't answer the phone. I knew she loved me like a daughter, but I'd hurt her son. I braced myself for a tongue lashing and touched the green button.

"Aunt Bobbie, hey!"

"Mabel, I'm disappointed." Okay, so much worse than a tongue lashing.

"I'msorry,I'msorry,I'msorry. I'm trying to figure out how to fix it," I rushed out.

"Sweetheart, fix what?"

"My relationship with Sam. Aren't you upset with me?"

"Only that it took you both so long to figure things out despite all the prep work your mom and I have done with you. The magic may have been acting quirky, but the basic premise remained the same."

"Aunt Bobbie, the magic almost drowned me." I gave my phone a dumbfounded look, as if my aunt could see me.

"Hmm, I suspect it hasn't aged well, but everything turned out all right in the end. I actually called to see how you were doing. I know you didn't suspect Sam's feelings for you."

She can say that again. "In hindsight, I should have had some idea. He was always such a good friend and never ever did anything to suggest otherwise."

"You probably weren't mature enough to recognize it."

"Gee, thanks." To be honest, she wasn't wrong, though I feel like I've aged a decade in the last week.

"Your mom and I had a powwow and have a theory."

Oh joy. "I can't wait to hear it."

"The magic has been with your family for a very long time, but at times, it seems to take on a life of its own."

"No kidding."

"It's always worked in the best interest for the women of your family, and I think maybe it's become invested. The magic was fulfilled when your parents married, and we haven't heard a peep from it. In fact, it should never have passed to you to begin with. It has always passed to the granddaughter at the death of the previous holder. Your mom and I guess that when one of Elizabeth's descendants makes poor decisions and fails to see what's right in front of her, it couldn't help but act. I think the magic is invested in preventing another Elizabeth-Danior situation."

"Who?"

Aunt Bobbie sighed on the other end of the connection. "The Gypsy man Elizabeth married instead of your dad's ancestor."

"Right. Sorry. There were a lot of names in the history, and it's not like I ever thought I'd need to know them."

"So, are you doing okay? I won't ask about your feelings for Sam. It's new for you."

"I'm just spending some time trying to figure some things out and give Sam time to be less mad at me."

"I'm sure he's not mad, just discouraged." That's worse than *disappointed*. Not helping.

"Hmm." I wasn't convinced. I needed practical advice, and the best place to get that was my sister.

Chapter 20

Horse sense

I hadn't spoken to Bertie in weeks. You know those cutsie coffee mugs that say, "my sister, my friend?" Yeah, we don't own a set of those. While not besties, Bertie and I have always served as reliable sounding boards for each other. If you want someone to not beat around the bush with their opinion, go to a sister. I helped her make a pros and cons list when trying to decide between art colleges in Atlanta and New York. She laughed at my pros and cons list when deciding on prom dates, then counseled me to choose the guy with the better reputation.

Every art teacher I've known has been easy-going and a bit flighty, in my opinion. In high school, I chose pottery for my fine arts credit. Mr. Randall was the type to find value in everyone's effort, even though my pot looked like a sad bedpan and exploded in the kiln when fired. Bless him for tolerating me.

But my sister is cut from a different cloth. Bertie graduated in the top five percent of her class and earned a full-ride scholarship to a prestigious Atlanta art college. She doesn't have a flighty bone in her body, except possibly the feather-light touch she applies to some of her pieces. She's two years younger and is the most practical artist I've ever known. With mixed feelings, I tapped the call button.

"Mabel. I'm heading to class soon. What do you need?"

I couldn't hear the love in Bertie's voice, but that was just her way. I figured I'd better cut to the chase. "Hey, Sis. Uh, have you talked to the 'rents recently?"

"No. Is something wrong?"

"Not with them. I've had some stuff come up that mom's aware of. I wondered if she'd warn—talked to you about it."

"All right. Spill and be quick."

I dove into the story from the beginning. She stopped me almost immediately.

"I don't believe you. Magic isn't real."

"You'd rather believe our parents, godparents, aunt, and uncle have all been lying to us for our entire lives?"

Bertie sighed. "I meant, it's not real anymore. Mom and Aunt Bobbie said it was finished."

"Mmm, not so much."

"Uh, I—never mind. Continue."

I continued the story of my time in *Love's Gamble*, with Bertie uncharacteristically quiet when she could have easily taken potshots at my stupidity. "Are you okay?"

"Of course. I'm just processing. So, what is your end goal?"

"Well, I want Sam back. He's my soul mate."

"You can't want him just because some expired magic said so. You didn't want him before."

"He's my best friend," I argued.

"He's your convenient friend. He's still the same Sam as before he became a sexy cowboy. Are you sure you want English Lit. major Sam? What do you bring to the relationship?"

I didn't have an answer to that. Already in my third year of school, I still hadn't declared a major, though my classes were trending toward history. When I wasn't in class, my work study job took most of my extra time. The school dining hall didn't inspire me to make any career choices in food service. "But he's loved me this whole time."

Bertie snorted. "No kidding, Einstein."

"What do you mean?" I began to wish I still had the horse to talk to.

"You are the only one oblivious to Sam's feelings for you."

"It wasn't that obvious," I retorted.

"Mom and Aunt Bobbie knew." She paused. "I knew," she said quietly.

"What's wrong?"

"Nothing. Just reminiscing. I had a crush on Sam for a lot of my teen years."

"You're barely out of your teen years."

"And I'm not pining after Sam anymore. I hated you so much sometimes. He was so into you, and you barely paid him any attention until you needed him to wipe your tears after a breakup. I finally realized that he would never see me as more than a pesky sister. It's fine. I'm over it, other than I'm still irritated with you for not appreciating him. He's still my friend."

"I need to figure out a way to get him back, apologize for years of ignorance, and declare my feelings once I figure out exactly what they are. I know cowboy Sam wasn't the real Sam, but what if it just allowed me to see him more clearly? We spent a lot of time together."

"Hmm," Bertie responded absently.

"Are you still listening to me? I swear your namesake was more attentive."

"Who? Not important. I'm mulling over your problem, but I've got some stuff of my own I'm dealing with."

Anything to take a break from my own problem. "Can I help?"

"Not at this juncture. What's your plan to convince Sam you're worth his time?"

"Rude! I'm thinking a grand gesture?"

"A what?"

"A grand gesture, like in romance novels. Go big or go home. You know?" I picked at a loose thread on the sofa arm while the thought germinated.

"I don't read fiction. I think Mom's stories scared me off it for a while and there's so much nonfiction I enjoy, I never went back."

"If you didn't create amazing art, I'd think you were the most boring person in the world."

"Um, thanks?"

"Sam quoted something while we were in the book. It was about friends and was really sweet. How about getting a tattoo similar to his. I need to prove to him I'm not his downfall. Did you know about his tattoo?" The idea sparked and took off like wildfire.

"Slow down. I knew he thought about getting one. He had me make up a couple sketches for him. How does it look?"

"I should have recognized your work. It looks good. Sexy."

"Ew. I can design you something similar if that's what you want to do. What's the quote?"

"It was really Englishy and said something about

friends and had the word betwixt in it. He didn't remember where it came from. I'll have to search it online and hope it's not too obscure."

"I know where it came from." I could hear the smirk in her voice. "You don't know about Sam's book, do you?"

And that clinched it. I was the worst friend in the world. Sam wrote poetry that got published and I never knew. Bertie seemed to relish telling me about Sam commissioning her to illustrate his and several other poems in a chapbook created by students in one of his graduate courses. I could buy it on Amazon or the campus online store. I looked it up while Bertie continued rubbing salt in my wound. Little brat.

"I've got to get to class. Let me know if you want my help with your tattoo." I could hear her moving around and her keys rattling in her apartment doorknob.

"Thanks for listening. I'll be in touch. Hey."

"Yeah?"

"Whatever you have going on, if you want to talk, I'm here for you." Bertie had been weirdly 'off' the entire conversation. Rude, yes, but far less snarky than usual.

"Sure. Bye." The line disconnected.

Chapter 21

...And didn't know it

I reserved a copy of Sam's book and picked it up at the campus bookstore on the way home the following evening. Sam and I attended the same local university but rarely ran into each other. It hurt that he'd never shared this accomplishment with me. Then, I tried to recall ever asking him about school. *I'm such a selfish witch. Ugh.*

The thin chapbook, titled *Odes and Lamentations*, taunted me from its bag in the passenger seat all the way to my apartment. I wanted to tear through it, anxious to learn what made Sam tick.

Snuggled up on my sofa with a glass of iced tea at hand, I cracked open the intriguing little book. I skipped over the forward and skimmed the table of contents. Sam wrote two, *My Passion, My Downfall* and *Unlonely Traveler*. The first was his tattoo. Did that mean the whole poem was about me? Oh dear.

I'm shadow cast. Her beauty, a shining beacon.
Russet and wild, a tempest unaware.

Yep, definitely about me. How embarrassing.

I'm absorbed completely, caught in orbit around her.
My own shining star,
My passion.
Along for the ride in the tumult of her existence,

She slams rudderless against stone after stone.
I, too, am beaten senseless,
Chewed up and discarded without ever leaving my
taste on her tongue.
My downfall.

I brushed moisture from my eyes. Is this what Sam thought of me? I only understood about three quarters of it—poetry wasn't my thing—but what I did get was bleak. My heart broke for us. Maybe the other poem was happier. The betwixt quote made it seem so. I hoped it wouldn't be about me, too.

Bump along a stoney path
Life of joy and life of wrath
Bear up, young man, have faith
For tis a journey, not a race
To endure sorrow and strife at times seem unjust
To equally savor good, dwell in bad, one must
Strength of heart and strength of friends
Betwixt the two, the future wends
Both are required for the term
When one falters the other holds firm
Feed one with truth and love and right
Gather friends as they incline toward your light
The two, when nurtured, will not fail
To advance your course despite assail

I found this one to be very poemy. I envisioned a medieval bard telling cryptic tales in dark ale houses along the English countryside. I got the gist, though. Basically, a person needs good friends and a strong moral compass to succeed, or possibly just make it through, life. I wanted to be that for Sam as he'd always been for me. This poem didn't sound like it was about me, but it still could be.

I flipped back to the first poem to study Bertie's illustration. Without the awkwardness of asking Sam to hold still while I ogled his tat, I could see more of the ink's intricate details. The trees and river growing and flowing from the open book were beautiful and, though the image was in black ink, it almost looked like the magic sparkles were alive. In contrast, the mountains were dark and shadowy with rigid cliff faces. I needed to find out who did Sam's tattoo. He'd copied Bertie's artwork precisely.

The image with the second poem was a curvy stream winding its way around rocks between two grassy banks until it disappeared at the horizon point. It would make a good shoulder tattoo with the quote running along the edge of the water. I'd get Bertie to make a few adjustments for me and add color.

Getting a tattoo would be the easy part. I still needed to plan how to present him with my grand gesture. I closed the book with a sigh…then immediately opened it again. Why wasn't I inside the book? Mom told me how my dad proposed inside a book of poetry. I scrambled off the sofa and crawled to the trunk filled with my family history junk I'd retrieved from my parents' house shortly after Sam and I returned. I peered in at the stacks of notebooks and typed pages. It'd be quicker to call Aunt Bobbie. With a sigh, I lifted out the topmost notebook.

"Gypsy magic 101, Mabel. You're stuck in the same book until it's over. Did you actually get to the end of the western?" my aunt asked.

"I thought we did since it sent us home." I glanced at *Love's Gamble*, still on the floor where I'd kicked it the night everything blew up.

"I bet there's an epilogue you missed. Only one way to find out," she said.

"I don't want to drag Sam back in and be stuck again for days." He'd hate me for that.

"Your mom and I were never gone longer than a few scenes. I don't know how you two were gone for a week but still didn't lose any time in the real world. I also don't know how Peter and I or your parents could only pop in briefly. Make sure you're taking good notes! You'll need to add all of this to the archive. I hope you're keeping everything safe."

The contents of the trunk were strewn all over my living room, because, yes, I tried to avoid calling Sam's mother. "It's all together and secure."

It looked like Sam, and I would be returning to the west. Crud.

Chapter 22

Spoiler, please

As I tried to ignore the constant buzzing that reminded me too much of a dentist's drill, I regretted requesting my tattoo be similar in size to Sam's. For one thing, my shoulder was smaller. I was afraid it would end up covering my entire back. And for another thing, ouch! It felt like the artist dragged a serrated knife across my skin. One or two seconds of drag, no problem; at about four seconds, I had to grind my teeth together to keep my body from flinching. I don't know why some people voluntarily did this to their whole bodies.

Four hours and a chunk of change later, I joined the ranks of the inked. I had what was essentially a permanent declaration of love blazoned across my shoulder. Even though it felt huge while I was getting it, the finished art only measured about four by five inches. As far as grand gestures went, I thought it served.

I still hadn't come up with a plan. I couldn't just whip my shirt off and display my tat like Sam did, though it might be the most direct way to get my point across. No. Being topless had the potential to backfire fantastically and maximize my embarrassment if Sam chose to reject me.

The more I thought about my conversation with Aunt Bobbie, the more sure I became that my grand gesture would have to happen inside *Love's Gamble*. But after that, I would swear off western romances forever. The only problem with my plan was that I had no idea how the story ended. Of course, I could be certain that Rose and her ranger somehow rode into the sunset and lived happily ever after.

At home that evening, I glared at *Love's Gamble* as if my scrutiny would force it to give up its secrets. There had been a love declaration, but since it came from Sam, it probably wasn't scripted. There were a couple more loose ends remaining to be tied. No dogeared pages or handy bookmark indicated where we exited the book. It felt like we were near the end, but there was no way to know for sure.

If, like Aunt Bobbie suggested, we merely skipped the epilogue, then Rose probably gets her closure regarding her relationship with Beau by letting him down easy. The end. But if there are several chapters remaining, for instance, if Jace kills the sheriff instead of being apprehended, it would effectively solve the Beau problem. Then there'd be another danger scene because of course the ranger would have to ultimately save the day.

"Argh! Why is this so complicated?" I slammed the book down on the sofa. I didn't want to drag Sam back into the book for more chapters, especially if he stayed mad at me. I needed to find out how the book ended. In this world where anyone could find out anything about anyone, surely it couldn't be that hard to—duh!

I grabbed my laptop from the coffee table and woke it up. My fingers flew across the keyboard, taking me to the best source of book details on the net—other readers. I pulled up all the book sale and review sites I could think of, anyplace with reader reviews. I scanned for the ones that warned of plot spoilers.

Forty-five minutes later I had enough information to understand the gist of how *Love's Gamble* ended…and to realize that my and Sam's intrusion into the plot caused the characters to miss out on some spicy scenes. My face warmed. If things went as I hoped, I'd get Sam to reenact some of those scenes with me in real life. Now, to plan my grand gesture.

****

Limiting my time spent with Mabel was easy. We didn't see each other too often during the week, anyway. Limiting my thoughts was another story, no pun intended. I wished we'd never gone into *Love's Gamble*; wished I'd never learned her true feelings.

I corralled my thoughts and turned my focus back to the essays I was grading for a first-year English class, but I could only read so many poorly written papers on the same topic before my mind began to wander again.

Ignoring the problem and my feelings wouldn't make them go away. At least not if Mabel and I would be thrown back together any time either of us opened a book. Goodbye all future plans for a career revolving around literature.

The question was, could we move forward from here? Would I be able to watch her go back to dating other guys? And with the soul mate bit, would it even be possible? I'd tried dating off and on over the years, but finally gave it up. Those women weren't who I wanted, weren't my destiny, apparently.

They say you don't get to choose your destiny, but what happens when your destiny doesn't choose you? I wouldn't be able to do it. I would graduate with my master's degree at the end of the semester, then I could move. There had to be a work-around for the reading into books thing.

One thing I was certain of, I couldn't see her. We couldn't continue to be casual friends and I didn't want the awkwardness of running into her all the time at family functions. My stomach turned at the thought of everyone's pitying looks.

I wanted Mabel to be happy, but I wanted me to be happy, too. And I couldn't do it by staying here.

Chapter 23

Home, home on the ranch
Love's Gamble

Ranger Cliff McGrath used his discarded shirt to wipe the sweat from his neck and chest before picking up the axe again. He'd already chopped two cords of wood to keep Rose through the winter. Maybe he should do another two or three just to be safe.

Rose may not be his, but he would see her taken care of for however long it took the sheriff to stake his claim. Cliff may have saved Rose's life, but the sheriff's capture of Jace Cutter ensured her continued peace of mind. Besides, a ranger's life wasn't suited for a wife or family.

With a swing of his axe, another log split in two. He wished abusing his body could take away the pain of losing Rose. His horse nickered, drawing his attention to an approaching rider on a familiar white horse. He turned away, swung, and split another log. He should leave well enough alone.

A glutton for punishment, Cliff grabbed his shirt and strode toward the ranch house. He held the damp article to his nose and decided donning it would offend Rose more than the sight of him shirtless. She ought to be used to him like that by now anyway.

The sheriff reached the porch and dismounted. He

untied a bruised bouquet of wildflowers from his saddle. Surely this wasn't how he planned to woo Rose. Cliff snorted with disdain. Beau hadn't noticed his approach from the backyard, so Cliff slipped into the shadow of the ranch house as he made his way to the front. He wanted to hear what the sheriff had to say to Rose. If Cliff found his offer unworthy of her, he'd have words with the man.

He heard the sheriff's boots on the front porch and his knock on the door.

"Sheriff Wilson, what a surprise. Whatever brings you all this way?" Rose was polite as ever. She'd make the perfect sheriff's wife, Cliff admitted to himself.

"Miss Rose, since a decent amount of time has gone since your folks passed and in light of recent events, I can no longer allow a single woman to live out here by herself. I wanted to court you proper, but I feel like we should forgo much of the formality in the interest of time and propriety."

"Is that so?" Cliff could hear the skepticism in Rose's voice. Why wouldn't she want to hitch up with the sheriff? He could give her everything Cliff couldn't.

"I've known from the moment I laid eyes on you two years ago that you were the woman for me. Rose, darlin', you'll make the perfect sheriff's wife and look mighty fine on my arm. Though you no longer have family connections, I'm willing to overlook that. Your fine character will help my career all on its own."

This guy's courtin' technique needed some work, Cliff thought.

"What's in it for me? All I'm hearing is how good I'll make you look," Rose replied. Cliff had spent enough time with her in recent days to know to be wary when

Rose's voice took on a certain tone.

"Like I said, it's not safe for a woman to live all the way out here by herself." Beau's tone held a touch of condescension.

"But you caught Jace Cutter. He's no longer a threat."

"There could be other threats and I don't like you being where I can't protect you."

"Are you saying I'd have to live with you in town?"

He continued with no sense of self-preservation. It made a man wonder how Beau could properly sheriff without any instinct. "Of course, married folk live together."

Cliff imagined Rose crossing her arms in a huff. "Is that your idea of a proposal, Beau Wilson? And what, pray tell, would happen to my farm?"

Cliff crept closer to the front of the house, anxious to see the expression on the sheriff's face when Rose gave him the set-down he deserved.

"Now Rose, I'll sell the ranch. You won't need it to make a living if you're married to me."

"You want to marry me so I'm not unsafe living alone, far from town, then you plan to sell the ranch that's been in my family for over a hundred years so I won't be living far from town anymore anyway?"

"I'm glad you understand, sweeting." Beau smiled, pleased Rose seemed accepting of the idea.

"I'll tell you what, you misogynistic, moronic, mall cop wannabe, that was the worst proposal I've ever heard in my life, and I've been propositioned with a dick pic before. You aren't half the man Sam is, and care more about your stupid fictional career than you do about me, er, Rose. If you really cared, you'd have been the first one in the water rather than riding off to catch the bad guy cause it would look better for your career."

Cliff frowned. He didn't understand most of what Rose said, but it sounded like she thought some other cowboy was better than the sheriff. He scratched at his beard only to meet with a smooth-shaven jaw.

The sheriff finally cottoned to Rose's anger. "I'm sorry you feel that way. I should have expected you to have formed an attachment to the land in a female sort of way. It will get easier with time. Once the young'uns come, you'll be too busy for ranching."

It was time to intervene. Cliff stepped the rest of the way out of the shadows. "Sheriff, you may want to consider pressing your suit another day or never." He turned to face the spitfire lady of the house. They needed to have a conversation, including why the heck Mabel had pulled him back into the book.

"Sam!" Thank goodness. Mabel practically leapt from the porch and threw her arms around me.

I set her back from me as soon as the hug ended. "What's going on? If you wanted to talk to me, you should have just called."

"You told me not to call." She pouted.

"Because I didn't want to listen to you make up excuses for my feelings. I laid my heart bare to you and you said nothing."

The sheriff chose that moment to remind us of his presence. "I see you've made your choice, Rose, but I can't help but believe it's the wrong one. I'm moving on. If you change your mind, it's unlikely I'll be available." He gave her one last aloof look before returning his hat to his head and climbing on his horse. He had one final line of script. "I hope you enjoy the life of a ranger's wife. You'll be just as alone as you've been these last six months." He rode to the edge of the yard before spurring his horse into a canter toward town.

"Good. I couldn't listen to his chauvinistic drivel any longer." She grabbed and held my hand. "I needed to be able to talk to you without you walking out. You caught me off guard before, and that's my fault for being so self-centered and oblivious to your feelings. In hindsight, I see all you've done for me, all you've been to me. The situation called for a grand gesture." She started unbuttoning the front of her dress.

"Whoa. Stop. What are you doing?" I put my hand over her fingers to stop their progress and registered my naked arm. "For cripes sake, where's my shirt?" At least my chest remained clean shaven this time. Mabel's gaze flicked to my waistband, and I found my shirt tucked there. It was damp and smelly, but I thrust my arms in the sleeves out of spite.

"I have something to show you," Mabel said as she returned to her buttons.

"Without your shirt?" I breathed a sigh of relief when only her chemise was revealed beneath her top.

She took my hands and met my gaze. "The magic isn't wrong. I see you, Sam, more clearly than ever before. I see all the parts to your whole. Well, maybe not all the parts, but I want to learn them all. My childhood best friend is still in there, along with the agreeable friend unknowingly trained to book-walk. You have the heart of a poet and the physique of an athlete. It all comes together into an amazing puzzle that I've come to realize I don't deserve."

"What?" My mind reeled at her honest observations.

"You've waited for me to stop being an idiot all this

time while I dated guy after guy and took advantage of your comfort when my relationships failed. I hurt you and I'm so sorry.

"The fact is, I'm not smart or clever. I don't have my life figured out. I'm selfish, I'm—"

I grabbed Mabel's shoulders. "Stop."

She hissed out a breath and shrugged away.

I pulled my right hand back. "What's wrong?"

"Nothing. Let me finish. I'm not good enough for you, but I think you're stuck with me, if the magic has anything to say about it. Everything just kind of hit me in the face like a baseball bat."

"Nice analogy. I'll alert Hallmark."

She frowned at me but continued. "I want to do better. I want a chance to deserve you. Sam, I want you. Please tell me it's not too late." Her eyes implored me.

I hated seeing her like this, doubting herself. "Mabes, you shine so bright. You were always my favorite person when we were kids. You've always been my person even when I gave you space to figure out what you wanted. I always wanted you to be happy, even if it meant you were with someone else. You're outgoing, brave, smart—" She shook her head. "Yes, smart. Maybe a little oblivious at times." I smiled, hoping to coax out her grin. "I've aways felt like I didn't deserve you. It kills me to hear you trash talk yourself because that's not what I see. It's never what I've seen. I love you."

"Sam," Mabel whispered and came into my arms.

She didn't have to say the words. Our relationship was changing. My heart pounded. I hadn't buttoned my shirt, and the lace of her chemise prickled my chest. "What's your grand gesture that requires disrobing?"

"Oh!" She slipped out of my arms and pulled her

arms out of her dress sleeves, allowing the bodice to hang from her waist. "I talked to Bertie. She told me about your poetry. Sam! How come you never said anything? Your writing is beautiful."

"You can probably guess why I didn't tell you. You weren't ready for my feelings, but I had to purge them someplace." I shrugged.

"Your tattoo. It's me, isn't it?" Her eyes dropped to the floor. "I don't want to hurt you anymore. I don't want to be anybody's downfall, least of all yours."

"The tattoo was a bit of an impulse. I'm sorry. I was hurting when I got it. You were never supposed to know. It was always to punish myself, never you." I'd get Bertie to redesign the thing if it would wipe the dejected expression from her face. "What's your grand gesture, Mabes?" I used a finger to raise her chin back up.

"Your poem, the other one, inspired me. You already have such a wonderful, strong heart. I want to be the friend on the other side to support you."

I closed my eyes and sighed. I needed to focus on the progress we'd made. She recognized that we'd eventually end up together, per the magic. If she needed us to start at the friend square again, I would.

"Sam? Are you even looking?"

I opened my eyes. Mabel had turned her back to me and pulled the armhole of her chemise, exposing the tattoo on her shoulder. It was still covered with a saniderm bandage, but I immediately recognized the artwork as Bertie's. Parts of my poem lined the banks of a rippling stream. "It's really beautiful. I'm honored." More than that, I was blown away.

Mabel turned back around with a huff. "You're not supposed to be honored. It's a declaration of love. It's my grand gesture. I've had a permanent symbol of my love for you carved into my skin. I love you, you dummy."

She really was perfect. She was the spark to set my dull life aflame and light up the shadowy recesses of my heart. My fingers twitched with the urge to put these feelings on paper. Later. The love of my life was waiting for a response. I scooped her up into a hug, being cautious of her shoulder. "Those are nearly the exact words I've dreamed of hearing." Though I'd dreamed about it for years, nothing prepared me for the thrill of finally pressing my lips to hers.

Chapter 24

The end, for now

Everyone milled around the backyard and patio as Uncle Tripp squeezed in one last cookout before the weather got cold and stayed that way. Even Mabel's sister, Bertie, made it home from school in Atlanta. The only difference between this afternoon and the hundreds of other occasions the Kinney and Celansky families socialized: Mabel's hand in mine.

I grazed my thumb across her finger; she turned her head and gave me a smile before continuing the conversation with her cousin. I loved the dress she'd chosen, a maroon sweater dress with shoulder cut-outs exposing the edge of her tattoo.

We'd always been best friends, despite the distance that came with age. Now, it was freeing to not have to hide my feelings. I didn't have to school my gaze from lingering too long or make up excuses to be near her. The intimacy of our new relationship status fit like a puzzle piece, completing a picture.

I cast away the poetic thoughts and refocused on my surroundings. Uncle Tripp, and Mabel's Uncle Gregorio argued over something on the grill while my dad looked on with an amused expression. Aunt Penny and my mom gave off strong meddling vibes as they carried on a serious discussion over by the drink cooler. Mabel's Aunt Kate chatted with Bertie while wiping the nose of her youngest child.

Upon wider perusal I saw the fire pit set up for stories and marshmallows later. The little-used trampoline sat off to the side of the backyard, and Uncle Tripp's archery targets looked a bit dilapidated backed up against the wooded part of the property. In the opposite corner, Mabel's old treehouse was barely visible among the colorful foliage still clinging to its tree.

I kissed Mabel on the temple and released her hand. "I'm gonna grab a soda. Want anything?"

She shook her head. "Not yet."

Skirting around my mom and aunt, not wanting to be drawn into their scheming, I pulled a root beer from the cooler. Wiping the wet can on my jacket, I walked along the back of the house and made my way to the treehouse.

Uncle Tripp kept it in good repair, as evidenced by two new ladder rungs. Mabel's younger cousins probably had as much fun up there as we used to. I gripped the rung, testing its strength, tucked the unopened can in my pocket, then hoisted myself up. The trapdoor banged open, and I fitted myself through the hole that seemed smaller than I remembered.

The inside smelled of new wood, suggesting the fresh floorboards had been placed recently. The rug looked new as well, but the faded curtains were exactly as I remembered. Beanbags had been replaced with two foam chairs which could be unfolded into a bed for a child—probably more comfortable than sleeping bags on the floor like Mabel and I did on occasion.

I leaned back against the wall and popped open my drink, letting the memories come. One day, Mabel and I would bring our kids here to play. I smiled at the thought and dragged the old chest closer, surprised it hadn't been removed.

The costumes inside were new, but a few faded bandanas looked familiar. More books were added to the stack. I pulled out the pirate one and freed the old eyepatch from where it had lodged between the cover and dust jacket, the broken elastic aged and no longer stretchy.

"Figures you'd be up here." Bertie's head poked up through the opening in the floor.

"Hey. I didn't hear you. I can leave." I guzzled the last of my drink and put the empty can back in my pocket.

Bertie climbed the rest of the way in. "No, you're fine. I just needed a break from the crowd."

"I thought you'd be used to the family chaos by now." I grinned.

"Living alone the last few months has spoiled me. What are you doing up here? Planning a honeymoon getaway for my sister?"

"When I take your sister on a honeymoon, it won't be anywhere the family can find us. I'm just airing out my memories. We had fun up here, didn't we?"

She gave me a wry grin. "When you actually let me play with you, I did."

I held up the pirate book. "Remember this? I know you played pirates with us."

She laughed. "You always made me walk the plank! But actually, I loved that part. The ocean was always a pile of pillows or leaves. Most of time I let you catch me." She frowned. "Until the last time."

I held up my hands. "We didn't mean for you to break your arm."

"What did you think would happen when you made me jump off the tree limb onto the trampoline?" She pursed her lips, but her eyes danced.

"It worked just fine when Mabel and I tried it first," I grumbled. "We were grounded from here until your arm healed. I'm sorry it happened, though."

She waved away my apology.

"I'll have to see if I can find a copy of this for my house for, well, kids someday. It was my favorite because it wasn't as girly as most of the others." I turned the book in my hands and opened the cover.

Bertie's eyes widened in panic behind her tortoiseshell frames. "Don't open it!"

I snapped it shut. "Why not?"

Mabel's head came up through the door in the floor. "That's where you guys are hiding! Dad sent me to find you all. Burgers are almost done." She climbed the rest of the way up and swung her bare feet through. I imagined I'd find her heels on the ground at the bottom of the ladder.

"Great! I'm starved." Bertie hurried down and out of sight before I could question her further.

Mabel rolled her eyes at her sister then turned to me. "Are you revisiting where it all began?"

Shrugging, I put the book and costume pieces back in the trunk. "It'd been a while. I wanted to see if the magic was still here."

She crawled over and sat next to me. "I think the magic is wherever we're together. But if you're asking if I want to climb into one of those old books with you, the answer is definitely no."

I wrapped my arm around her shoulders and pulled her close. "Feeling a little book-shy?"

"I'm just wondering when I'll be brave enough to try to read anything other than an audiobook or my chemistry and math texts."

"The lore is clear about what will solve your problem," I whispered into her ear.

"I remember, but I'm not in that big of a hurry. I want to enjoy you, us, like this for a while. We have the rest of our lives to do the married thing and all that goes with it. I want it and look forward to it, but I want to make great memories of this time, too. I suppose it's to make up for the regret of not realizing it sooner. Is that okay? Am I making sense?" She looked at me, her expression hesitant.

"Of course. I'm not trying to rush you." I kissed the top of her head. "I love the way this feels, too. After so long, it doesn't quite seem real to me yet. I'm happy enjoying now with you and knowing you're my future."

Mabel sniffed, and when she turned her head, a tear trickled down her cheek. She climbed onto my lap, facing me and wrapped her arms around my torso, clinging like a barnacle. "I love you, Sam. I can't wait for everyday with you."

As the smell of grilled burgers filtered through the air, I returned my true love's embrace. *Thank you, gypsy magic.*

A word about the author...

Shelley is a twenty-five year resident of Oklahoma with roots in Maine. She and her husband have four awesome kids and three dogs. She spends her time writing, reading, baking, sewing, and exercising just enough to counteract her other activities.

The In for a Penny Series was inspired by penny idioms.

www.ingramcontent.com/pod-product-compliance
Lightning Source LLC
Chambersburg PA
CBHW060121260626
47160CB00005B/1970